Let Me Count the Ways

This book is dedicated to Anna.

LET ME COUNT THE WAYS

Deborah Bosley

C

CENTURY · LONDON

This edition published by Century Books Limited 1996

1 3 5 7 9 10 8 6 4 2

Century
20 Vauxhall Bridge Road, London, SW1V 2SA

Arrow Books Ltd
20 Vauxhall Bridge Road, London, SW1V 2SA

Random House Australia (Pty) Limited
16 Dalmore Drive, Scoresby,
Victoria 3179, Australia

Random House New Zealand Limited
18 Poland Road, Glenfield
Auckland 10, New Zealand

Random House South Africa (Pty) Limited
PO Box 2263, Rosebank 2121, South Africa

Random House UK Limited Reg. No. 954009

A CIP catalogue record for this book is available from the British Library

Papers used by Random House UK Limited are natural, recyclable products made from wood grown in sustainable forests. The manufacturing processes conform to the environmental regulations of the country of origin.

ISBN 0 7126 7751 8

Typeset by Palimpsest Book Production Limited,
Polmont, Stirlingshire
Printed and bound in Great Britain by
Mackays of Chatham plc, Chatham, Kent

PART ONE

FRANCES SLEPT FOR thirteen hours and woke up struggling for breath in the small room. The sun dazzled through the gaps in the blinds as she tried to open her eyes and she felt a bit sick. Her head was heavy with the wine and sleeping pills of the night before and her characteristic remorse began to well up. She muttered 'Oh fuck' and pushed down the bedclothes that were smothering her. Through the walls she could hear the sounds of American life being played out – hysterical audience laughter boomed from the TV, the air-conditioner hummed down the hallway and the automatic garage door creaked shut as her mother-in-law's silver Pontiac crunched across the gravel and out of the yard.

The heat of her narrow bedroom was stifling and she lay perfectly still, unable to get up and open a window. Frances watched the shadows of trees moving across the walls and counted on her fingers the number of days she had been in Dexter – seventy-one. Slowly she began to stretch and scratch, moving each limb heavily, as if through water, until her feet came to rest on the carpet; her small body slumped down between her legs until she could lift her head and look across at her reflection in the mirror opposite. Her face was puffy and beneath her tan she looked drawn and pale. Matted hair clung in sweaty clumps across her head. 'Great,' she told herself and got up.

She padded down the hallway into the brilliance of a white kitchen flooded with sunlight and opened the refrigerator, standing for several minutes to let the cool air move across her body. She pulled out a bottle of cranberry juice and drank down its contents in one, slaking the thirst that had woken her. The juice sent the previous night's alcohol coursing through her one more time; she felt light-headed and, for a brief moment, happy. In the barely-cool of the air-conditioned lounge the TV was blaring to nobody, the porch door was open and fine curtain fabric billowed in the breeze. Frances stepped outside onto the wooden deck, into a different warmth and saw her husband; he lay in the shade with a thin cotton blanket over his legs, a magazine hanging lazily from his hand. His eyes were closed and his mouth hung open to show a small white streak of saliva across the bottom lip. 'Finn,' she croaked, her words catching in the fur and congestion of too many cigarettes; then clearing her throat, louder this time, 'Finn . . .'

He opened one eye and looked at her. 'So you made it up before lunch,' he said, 'how are you feeling?'

'Not bad,' she lied, sinking down sideways on the lounger next to his and patting his forearm – skinny now, but still with its thick silken hair.

'I heard you crashing around in the night,' he said, 'did you have fun?' Both eyes open now, he looked at her, a slight smirk playing on his face.

She studied his face for several seconds and decided she didn't have the stamina for an argument; besides, he wasn't baiting her, just enjoying the spectacle.

She yawned and scratched her head. 'I don't know what's the matter with me. I spend all day wishing I were in bed and all night wide awake. Sorry if I kept you up.'

'Yeah well, cheap wine will do it to you every time,' he said, turning back to his magazine.

'It stops me turning over the same things, again and again in my mind.' Her words were blurred by a yawn. Acid rose noisily in her stomach.

'What things?' he asked, not really wanting to hear her answer.

'Us,' she said. He made no response. He was good at

starving an unwelcome topic. She didn't want to talk about it either, but went on anyway.

Stretching out, she gazed down the yard to the pond in the distance where the Webber girls from the house across the way were shrieking in their dinghy. 'I don't know what's the matter with me, I never used to be like this. I suppose things are different now, or at least I am.'

'I guess so . . .' He had his thoughts about this, but suspecting the blame might lay somewhere with him, kept them to himself.

'Look Finn, forget it. I'll take a shower and if you're feeling up to it, we'll drive out somewhere for lunch.'

'Which part of the corn belt is it exactly that calls?'

Frances didn't like his tone but resisted the irritation. 'Oh I don't care, anywhere. Any small town – Ypsilanti, Chelsea, Ann Arbor . . .' She paused. 'Anywhere that isn't here. Just some life, people, anything really . . .' she trailed off, still looking at the girls in their boat, screeching and laughing, their bright swimsuits dancing on the relentless green of the pond and the surrounding trees, unaware that they wouldn't always feel so gay, or of the sorrow that looked like two ordinary people sitting on their deck.

She tried to remember what she had felt like at their age and concluded that it must have been good. She used to laugh all the time – or at least that was how it seemed from the distance of adulthood – mostly about boys. She had been a teasing, boisterous girl who developed precocious habits to overcome her smallness. A wiry, lippy creature who smoked and shoplifted, determinedly becoming one of the girls. She hadn't cared then that boys never asked her to dance because she knew she was popular anyway and would probably get taller. She was certain that when she grew up, say twenty-five, she would meet a man and fall in love. And she did. She had thought that she would find a man who was different and special, not like the others. Someone who would find her rare and fascinating. And she had. She just hadn't bargained on it being such a drag.

She slouched, staring at the girls on their boat, while her husband studied her profile, noting the changes. She still wore a long fringe which masked her swollen brown eyes but the mouth, once small and soft, had set in a line. So petulant. She wore a puckered look of frustration which altered her lovely face into an accusation. He felt its reproach. 'You miss London don't you?' he said, 'why don't you go home?'

Frances didn't move a muscle, but his words stirred her out of her funk and she answered him. 'Because I want to be here with you.'

'But I'll manage doll, I've got mom,' he said.

'Do you want me to leave?' She turned to look at him, to see his eyes when he answered her.

'No I don't. It's good to have you here, I mean it.' He managed a half-smile, but he was weak, sweating even in the cool of the shade. Frances fussed about, looking under the lounger for the cigarettes she had left there the night before. He hated her smoking and when she lit the cigarette she did so without looking at him. 'Even if you do smell like a poolhall most of the time,' he said lightly. She smiled up at him, softly blew a plume of smoke in his face and began to laugh.

'Goddamnit Fran . . .' he choked and coughed, his face turning a deep shade of red and his eyes watering. Frances' defiance waned when she heard the looseness in his chest, the deep whine that emanated as he inhaled between coughs.

'Oh God Finn, I'm sorry, I forget,' she said, stubbing out her cigarette.

'Jeez, I wish I could,' he said drily.

He had given up being censorious with his wife. It was easier to let her amuse him from a distance, refusing to allow her swift changes of temper to touch him. He lived quite alone these days, it was his time; Frances could exist from the sidelines. It was good to have her around, but not inside, where she could get to him again. She searched his face for signs of anger and found none.

'I'll go and take a shower then,' she said.

'Whatever.'

They left the house around noon and Frances steered the Oldsmobile out of the dirt roads surrounding the squat wooden houses. They drove slowly down the highway, crossed a bridge over the Huron River and followed its course along miles of empty riverbank, shaded by the tall cottonwoods and poplars. Dappled light fell through the trees and danced across the highway. Beyond the riverbank, miles of corn reared up and dropped in the breeze. It was cooler now, the air had started to move, so Frances switched off the air-conditioning and opened the windows of the car.

The wind had been uncertain for days, hidden somewhere; blowing in some other county – moving corn in Ohio maybe. She would sit on the deck in the dark and wait for a breeze to come and take away the scent of dying flowers. Fireflies would dart around her head and dogs would bark, but nothing could move the air. Only in the dead of night, if she woke up and stepped outside, could she feel a chill, something familiar. The dogged persistence of the heat was getting her down. She was English, she needed the rain.

As the car picked up speed, air blew through, lifting her hair and raising goosebumps on her skin. She lit a cigarette and mused to herself that smoking while driving had to count as one of her greatest pleasures; she smoked a stale, sun-baked cigarette halfway down before asking him if he minded.

'Does it matter?' he shouted above the noise of the engine. She smiled and sped along a dead straight course of the river road, her eye on a bend up ahead. They touched hands briefly, Frances relaxing into his approval.

There were still moments when she entertained him, when a glimpse of her forgotten insouciance helped him remember what it was he had seen in her. That heedless spark that made him think she could turn his life around, that he could learn from her not to care so much. He sometimes hoped she might find again her ease, the light touch with which she'd moved him. It was too late now, and even if they had more time they both knew they'd lost something which could never be recovered. Frances had yet to come to terms with this knowledge.

Still it was good to be out of the house. He felt no worse than usual and it was a beautiful day; the humidity level was down. They were happy just to keep driving for a while, passing through the small settlements, with their farms, general stores, gas stations and one stoplight. Frances would turn off and take the bridges over the Huron, crisscrossing back and forth to the highway again. The bridges were old and made a great noise as they drove across. Painted loud shades of pink, red, green and black their wooden boards spanned the muddy waters that rushed beneath. As Frances drove she looked around and tried to take in everything; these were precious days after all.

Frances didn't want to go back to London, not yet. She hadn't worked out what she'd do if she returned. She certainly wasn't ready to face her life again, not until she'd finished dealing with this one. She would stick around for a while and see what happened. As lost as Frances felt in Michigan, she at least had a reason to be there; there was nothing and nobody waiting for her back home. Besides, she appreciated the change of location. If London was her home – and she wasn't sure that it was anymore – it had become an inhospitable one. Although there seemed to be fun going on around her, she felt excluded from its comforts. There she had perfected the social kiss, only to find herself trapped within its etiquette. She had wanted to escape, to be in the middle of nowhere for a while. She had come to the right place.

Before she arrived, she had studied her map of Michigan and noticed how the state was the shape of an oven mit. Her destination, Dexter, was a small town – a cow town as it was known locally – which sat in the left-hand corner of Washtenaw County. It was an insignificant agricultural settlement of around three thousand people with some half-decent real estate. Detroit, Michigan's capital lay only an hour and a half along Interstate-94 from Dexter – about four inches on the map – but as soon as she got to Dexter she could see that city life was a long way away.

During the boom years of the forties, fifties and sixties, Detroit had been the prosperous centre of the automobile industry. In decline for the last twenty or so years, its urban blight was redeemed in flashes only by the Palladian columns of its museums and the soaring modern towers of downtown. When Frances had first arrived from London – an event which prompted something of a revival for Finn – they drove into Detroit and took the glass elevator to the thirty-second storey of the Cultural Center. They stepped out into a revolving bar which served big drinks and offered views across the Detroit River to Canada, revealing the city as it turned. She had felt excited by her surroundings, soaking it all in and thinking that her world was opening up, albeit in strained circumstances. Even the slums of Detroit had a tough glamour – where there were once fancy stores and grand mansions, there remained only boarded-up crack houses and fortified loan shops. It made a change.

Dexter had experienced neither boom nor bust; life had been the same for as long as anybody could remember. There were people in Dexter who had never been to Detroit in their whole lives and expressed no desire to go there. A white, hardworking, God-fearing community of Irish and Norwegian sod-busters, they kept their barns tidy and their children clean. Limited though it surely was, Dexter became

Frances' whole world, and for the time being at least, it was enough. She didn't want to travel, she didn't think there was time. Her husband never wanted to go further than another room in the house, so Frances would set off by herself in the afternoons and study the town. She knew which side of Main Street fell into shade first and what time the K-Mart closed. The shopkeepers eyed her curiously, but accorded her friendly respect; they might comment on the weather or say 'You take care now' when they handed her some change, but nothing more. Something about the whiteness of their skin and their neat, simple lives made Frances feel safe – insulated even from the big sick joke that her life had become.

According to her husband, Dexter people were Republicans who rarely smoked or entertained liquor in their homes. They didn't lock their doors either, but usually packed a rifle in their closets. The men were solid from hard work and their women benign with domesticity. The good people of Dexter were intrigued by Frances, but their own good manners, and Frances' strict instructions from her mother-in-law to share their business with nobody, kept things on nodding terms only. Neighbours and friends of the family – such as they were – didn't even know that Homer Finney had a wife until Frances came from England, but they'd always known there was something odd about him. He had been a loner who went to college in Los Angeles – most Dexter students elected to study at Ann Arbor, only fifteen miles away. As a boy, he had never played football with the other sons of Dexter and this had been enough to single him out as strange.

The womenfolk smiled politely when they passed Frances in the aisles at Meyers, and took care to see what it was she was putting in her shopping cart. They thought she seemed pretty friendly, but didn't like to pursue it. To these honest women, she was unfathomably exotic and sophisticated. Small, dark and usually dressed in black, she appeared impossibly dainty next to the strong, corn-fed, local females. Dexter was a town full of sturdy people with capable hands. Somebody was always building, fixing or baking something. Frances would shake her head and laugh at the film-fantasy of water towers and general stores, grain silos and children roaming freely. In Dexter, folk really did wash their cars on Sunday after chapel and say Grace before a meal of boiled chicken and grits.

Frances was the most exciting thing to hit Dexter since the Episcopalian preacher, Brendan O'Connor, had his nervous breakdown and admitted to an affair with Ginger Olson. There had been rumours when Finn had returned home the year before, but Meg Finney had been stoic and confided in nobody. The arrival of a wife really whipped up local talk, and the suspicion that Homer Finney had cancer was not one his mother was at pains to kill. He didn't seem to be working, he never left the house. That Frances had persuaded him to do so that day – to get in the car and go somewhere – was a small triumph for her. Unusually, she felt at ease, knowing that in small ways, he still wanted to please her by letting her wishes prevail.

As they drove, all thoughts of lunch disappeared – they couldn't waste such a beautiful afternoon sitting indoors someplace and Frances cursed herself for not packing a picnic. She wanted to wring every last second out of this rare and good day. She kept driving. She worried that if she stopped the car, the spell would be broken and their customary tension would resume. What a godsend it was to have Meg's old car just sitting in the drive. She bought the Pontiac for herself on a good finance plan when Finn had arrived from San Francisco. She thought he could use the old one, but he hadn't been able to drive for months. They moved along the southern bank of the Huron River, wide and empty, making no sound. When she turned off the radio, the only noise was of a warm breeze moving through the open windows of the brown Oldsmobile. They spent about two hours doing this – just driving around. Frances turned to share a comment about the temperature of the water – maybe they could take a swim – and saw Finn asleep. His face had lost all its colour and the skin covering his eyelids seemed thin, as if it would split. She crossed over Ypsilanti bridge and made the loop across the highway for home.

Frances was standing in the kitchen flaking fish for supper and whistling to a tune on the radio when her mother-in-law's car arrived in a cloud of dust at the back of the kitchen where the drive curved into the yard. She climbed out of the Pontiac – a sports model unsuited to a woman of her years, Frances thought – and walked around the house to the front of the breakfast room to check the grain in the bird feeder. Frances watched her through the window. Under one arm she had a pile of books and over the other was slung a white leather bag. Large sunglasses rested on the top of her silver-grey head and reflected the low sun. Her outfit was the ill-fitting assortment of colours and fabrics that passed for a lively dress sense in Dexter. White cotton trousers, through which could be seen the hue of her underwear, were topped with a yellow knitted short-sleeved sweater with a red trim around the collar and sleeves.

As her mother-in-law turned to come into the house, she saw Frances standing at the window and waved. She opened the front door to let a bright arc of light fall across the hall, and a sudden gust of wind swept through it, slamming shut the light wooden doors of the downstairs bedrooms, where Finn and Frances slept. His mother slept upstairs.

'Hello Meg,' said Frances.

'Hey Frankie, how're you doing,' she said. 'Where's Homer?'

'Sleeping. Kedgeree OK for dinner?' She continued flaking the fish, putting the fine bones on a dish.

‘Sure. What is it?’ The older woman screwed up her face in enquiry.

‘Fish and rice with some egg and parsley – plain enough for Finn?’ Frances’ mother-in-law was convinced that a plain diet could cure all sickness.

‘So what did you kids do today?’ She asked, sorting through the pile of books she had put on the table. She didn’t wait for an answer. ‘Cindy gave me some great titles. Let’s sit down after dinner tonight and go through them.’ Her nose was already firmly between the covers of *Betty Shine’s Mind Workbook*.

‘Well, I’m a bit tired, we went for a long drive along the river today. We were gone for hours, the time went so quickly,’ said Frances.

Her mother-in-law looked up with interest. ‘Oh you did? How great, it was a beautiful day with that breeze. Is Homer sleeping?’

‘Yeah. He’s done in now, but I think it did him some good to get out of the house.’

‘Sure,’ said the older woman quietly, studying her daughter-in-law before returning to her book.

‘Meg, I’m going to go to Meyers, do you want anything? I know we’re out of rice,’ Frances lied.

‘Oh honey, there’s some in the dry store, you don’t want to go all that way. Anyway, it’s going to storm tonight, have you listened to the weather reports on the radio?’

‘No,’ Frances said, looking out of the window to see a cluster of dark clouds that looked only a little threatening.

‘Well, Ohio had bad electric storms last night and about four inches of rain. I wouldn’t advise it, honey.’

Frances felt irritation building. They both knew the real reason for her wanting to go to the store. The night before, Frances had finished what was left of the half-gallon bottle of wine which she had stored at the back of the cupboard under the kitchen sink, away from scrutiny. The prospect of getting through an evening listening to her mother-in-law reading from self-help books, unaided by a drink, was more than she could stand. She knew that Meg wasn't unaware of this. But she didn't know that her mother-in-law checked the cupboard under the sink every morning though. Meg smiled warmly at her daughter-in-law and came over to give her a hug. Frances bristled under her touch and pulled away. 'You know, it's really great that you're here for Homer, Frances, I really appreciate it.'

Frances didn't speak, just turned up the corners of her mouth and went to get cleaned up for dinner.

Finn slept through dinner and Frances ate in silence while Meg studied her pile of books. She would look up occasionally to urge them on her daughter-in-law. 'Honey, you must read this, it's so great,' she said of *Good Grief – Coping with Bereavement*. Frances loaded the dishwasher and wiped the surfaces feeling edgy and wishing she had a glass of wine. The threatened storms hadn't materialized yet, though clouds filled up the sky, seeming to throw a blanket over the day's merciful breeze, and the humidity shot up once more signalling some rain. Frances took her cigarettes from her bag and dragged a wicker chair out onto the deck to put some space between herself and the woman in the kitchen. Thinking that Frances was observing the smoking ban in the house, Meg called out, 'I really appreciate it Frankie.'

'No trouble,' Frances called back, and picked up the *New Yorker* that Finn had been reading earlier in the day, its pages crisp and crackling from exposure to the sun. She couldn't stand the *New Yorker* – as a restless girl she found its articles too long, but she sustained the appearance of concentration so an idle moment wouldn't be mistaken for an opportunity to talk.

By 9 p.m. it was closer still, there wasn't a breath of air. Frances' cigarette smoke hung static around her as she exhaled, and her skin itched. The faint smell of withered jasmine came and went and the noise of the crickets seemed to fade. The quiet was interrupted by their neighbour across the wide pond, rippling the water as he tied up the small boat his daughters had been playing in earlier. Chip Webber was a nice man from what Frances could make out: a dentist. Behind him, she could see figures that she presumed to be his wife and daughters, moving around in their kitchen. It was a simple scene that depressed her profoundly. She envied them their routine security and wondered how different things might have been between her and Finn.

She didn't hear Meg step onto the deck and was shaken out of her dreamy observations only when she heard, 'Iced tea Frankie?' She started with a jump and looked up to find Meg fixing her with that look she had come to recognize as a prelude to intimate conversation.

'Um, yeah, why not,' Frances replied, before stiffening and sitting up straight in her chair. She had come to dread these little talks, when her mother-in-law would join her on the deck and try to get to the bottom of Frances' supposed problems – her distance and sadness. That the reasons for them were not obvious astounded Frances.

She heard the ice-cubes in the plastic beakers make their progress across the lounge and out onto the deck where it was dark now, lit only by lights from within the house, casting long shadows. Meg handed Frances her drink and pulled a lounger over to where she sat. Frances took a deep breath, inhaling the powdery fragrance that her mother-in-law favoured, and said by way of stalling the inevitable, 'Nice scent'.

'Why thank you,' Meg replied, momentarily abashed before going on. 'You know, these books that Cindy gave me are just wonderful. I think this one is really neat.' She waved a copy of Roberta Wurman's *Thoughts For the Soul* at Frances.

Unable to raise a flicker of interest but asking politely, Frances said, 'Why, what does it say?'

Encouraged, the older woman spread the book on her knees and with her solid, work-worn hands turned the pages, looking for something she had in mind for her woeful daughter-in-law. 'Here it is, "If you have any compulsive or co-dependent behavior patterns, ask yourself, 'What for?'"' She paused here to look at Frances, but Frances wouldn't catch her eye. She went on, '"If you stopped what do you think would happen to you? Of course, people say, 'I would be stronger, life would be better.' Don't you think you deserve a sweeter life, do you have problems with self-esteem?"' An awkward pause hung heavy between them, and Frances felt it incumbent upon her to make some response. She fidgeted, lit another cigarette and turned to look at Meg.

'I'm sorry, was that directed at me or were you just reading it aloud for the purpose of debate?' Embarrassed, Meg looked down at her book and flicked some pages. She didn't like Frances' sarcasm.

'Well, I think it applies to all of us Frankie, but you're so young and I can't help noticing that you have these negative habits. You smoke and drink and it seems such a waste. Leastways it doesn't seem to make you happy.' Meg's words tumbled out, half explanation, half apology.

Frances felt her usual twinge of guilt. Why was she so hard on this woman – she was only trying. Misguided and irritating maybe, but not an evil woman; not a woman possessed by the dark thoughts that Frances found herself prey to. Without establishing the eye contact which Meg favoured, Frances reached across and took her mother-in-law's rough, broad hand in her own small one. 'Look Meg, I know you mean well, but it isn't the smoking and drinking that make me unhappy . . . they're just habits.' She would have said more, but Meg was poised with a revelation and interrupted:

'I know, I know, but they're a symptom of your unhappiness, honey. Just because things didn't work out with Homer, you don't have to keep punishing yourself.' Frances looked at her, briefly delighted by an image of herself whacking Finn around the head, and asked with a laugh, 'You think I should punish him instead?'

Now she was confused. Meg's hand flew to her head where she twisted the coarse silver hair between her fingers. 'No, that's not what I mean Frances. You have to heal yourself; there's something here that says it better than I can.' She scoured the book for another pearl. 'Here it is. "Go ahead, waste your life dwelling on the negativity, thinking of all the things that went wrong. But wouldn't it be wonderful if you could love yourself and think about all the beautiful experiences you've had? Thinking positive, joyful thoughts is the only way to create a healthful, fulfilling life." Isn't that wonderful?' Meg finished on a pleading note. She snapped the book shut and looked at Frances hopefully.

Frances found it hard to remember if she had ever heard anything so crass in her life. She was sickened by her mother-in-law's supermarket philosophy, but touched by the outstretched hand that came with it. Despite the rebuffs which Frances always fired back, Meg kept trying. Would it really be so difficult to indulge the poor woman, to let her think that she was a comfort and a help? Frances spoke with deliberate care.

'You know how difficult the English find it to digest these sentiments, Meg. Emotion just isn't our natural language, we don't have the facility with it that Americans seem to.' Disarmed by what she thought was a compliment, Meg softened and shuffled closer so that she might clutch Frances' bony shoulders and look into her eyes.

'You know Frances, coming here after everything that has happened was a positive step, but you need to close the circle and move on. You can't keep reliving the negativity. What's going on here is sad but when it's all over, you have your life ahead of you. You'll meet somebody else, it'll be different.' Meg squeezed her hands tighter as she watched Frances' eyes fill up with tears. 'Oh Gosh, now I've upset you.'

'No, no, it isn't you. I just can't stand to watch him like

this, Meg. When will it end?' Frances pulled away from Meg's hands and covered her eyes with her own in a bogus display of emotion – the tears were not for him.

'I don't know honey, but you don't have to stay. Why don't you go home?' For the second time that day Frances heard herself say, 'Do you want me to leave?'

'No, no I don't and neither does Homer, but look what it's doing to you,' said Meg.

Frances sniffed and took a deep breath, composing herself. 'It'll be OK, I'll pull myself together.' Then, wiping her eyes, 'You're sweet to worry.'

Meg nodded sympathetically and put the book on Frances' lap before getting up and walking back into the house, sighing.

For a few minutes Frances just stared at the cover with its rainbows, bluebirds, hearts and flowers and thought that if she had a drink she might even find this evening funny. A change of company could also make a difference. It would be good to talk to somebody. She couldn't call home because Meg, as the only wage earner, could not afford to pay international phone bills and Frances couldn't afford to contribute much. If her situation was hard to bear even with the friend that drink had become, sober it was impossible. Heat lightning lit up the sky in random bursts, but still the air didn't move. She could have gone to the store after all, there wouldn't be any storms tonight, just as there hadn't been a drop of rain for the last ten weeks.

Elmo, the old collie waddled out of the lounge across the deck and down the steps that led into the yard. After raising his leg and spraying one of the squat little bushes that surrounded the base of the deck, he struggled back up the steps and nuzzled Frances' hand, before he too disappeared inside the house. This small act of tenderness made Frances weep again; what a dreadful evening this was. She opened the book in the middle and found emblazoned across a page, 'Be conscious of what's in your mind at this very moment, this thought is the foundation of your future. Is it a joyful or a negative thought? Are you sure you want your life to be built around this?' Frances snorted and turned the page to find, 'Take comfort from the fact that you are never alone, never abandoned. You are pure consciousness, at one with the universe. You are whole.' She slammed the book shut and muttered to herself, 'Jesus Christ.'

Unable to sit there on that deck with either her thoughts or the little book for a minute longer, Frances got up and went inside to look for the sleeping pills she had secreted away from Finn's supply.

When Frances woke, tears were pricking her eyes and her limbs felt stiff and heavy. In her stomach was a dull ache and her head was pounding. For once the drink wasn't to blame and she knew that the tightness across her forehead was due to the cyclical anger and emotion that would dog her for a week or so before she bled. Last month, Meg had tried to cure her ills with vitamin supplements and a total ban on coffee and alcohol. She didn't share her mother-in-law's view that monthly depression could be cured by healthy living and a regulated diet. Nature, she knew, had its way of symptomizing the miserable failure to conceive. Frances felt doubly chastened by the knowledge that her husband could never give her the child she felt was her right. It had always been an impossibility, but at least she hadn't known that in the beginning.

Across the hall she could hear Meg speaking with Finn and fetching him tea before she went to work. 'You should really try and eat something in the mornings, it's not good just to drink tea and coffee all day, you'll get sick to your stomach.'

'Mom, it's because I feel sick to my stomach that I can't eat, I'd rather feel empty than nauseous.' There was a suggestion of a whine in his voice.

'Dr Craig said that you should eat plain foods if you want to get well.'

'Dr Craig's an ass, I'm not going to get well.'

'Don't say that sweetie; you will, but you must eat. Let me open these curtains.' In his mother's voice there was hectoring tone.

'Mom, leave it, don't worry OK, go to work, I'll be fine. Frances will be up soon.'

'Well, I sure hope she is, I don't know why she sleeps so much, I've never seen a girl her age like it, it's crazy.'

'Mom, it's all right, don't worry.'

'OK baby, I'll be back around four this afternoon.' Frances heard Meg kiss her son and her stout heels click down the hallway and through the kitchen, then the back door opened and closed.

Frances lay in bed and listened to the car pulling out of the yard before crossing the hallway into Finn's room. The curtains were drawn and the windows open, but no breeze stirred within. The room was hot and had the sickly, milky smell of decay. Beneath the loose covers Finn's chest rose and fell heavily with effort and his brow was covered in sweat. His eyes were pinched tightly shut like those of a child making a wish over a birthday cake, and he was speaking softly to himself. This was real pain, not the vague awfulness that Frances was feeling. Then her recurring and shaming conviction that he only had himself to blame for the state they were both in rose again and blocked any real compassion that might have swollen inside her.

'Finn, what's the matter?' she asked sharply. He didn't stir from his mumblings, so she sat on the bed, pushing aside the old dog who was nuzzled against his chest, and took his hands in hers. She had picked up the habit of touching from her mother-in-law. She was shocked at how cold he felt. The fingers were white except for the knuckles which were an angry red and she squeezed them softly, rubbing them and trying to put some warmth back. 'Finn?' she asked, her anger diffusing into guilt. He blinked in a cartoon fashion, scrunching his eyes up tight and opening them wide several times before looking at her.

'Hey girl,' he croaked and smiled to reveal the yellow teeth that he never bothered to brush anymore. A fine madness danced in his green eyes, rimmed with crust. His former fastidiousness had enchanted Frances. She would watch him in the mornings, flossing his teeth and brushing them carefully, between shaving, taking his shower, combing his hair and dressing. These days it was hard to get him near a bath. Frances felt the sheet that lay across him and was startled to find how wet it was.

'Do you want to get up so I can put some fresh linen on for you?' she asked.

'No, I think I'll just lie here for a bit . . .' he trailed off and closed his eyes again.

'Did you sleep okay?' she asked rhetorically. He opened his eyes and looked at her closely for several seconds, studying the tired face and doleful expression.

'Oh, I think I grabbed a couple of hours between three and six this morning, mostly I was too busy just sweating. The Halcyons don't seem to work anymore. Jesus, Frankie, I'm so tired of this.'

She had no thoughts on this subject, or at least none worth stating. He shifted uncomfortably in the bed, trying to sit up; Frances put her hands under his arms to lift him but he pushed her away feebly. 'It's OK, I can do it,' he protested.

'I'm sorry, it just looked like a real effort for you.'

'It's OK, it's OK, just leave me alone for a while, huh? Everything's a goddamned effort. I'll get up for lunch . . . It looks like a beautiful morning out there, you should get out and enjoy it.' He patted her hand, comforting the child. 'I'll be fine, just some water would be good.'

Relieved that there was this one small task she could do for him, she fetched his water and put on a smile when she came back into the room. She could at least pretend that she didn't feel lousy too. 'I think I'll take the dog out and then go to the store. I trod on my sunglasses the other day, I need a new pair. I should get something for lunch as well, what do you fancy?'

'Oh, a coupla Martinis and some steak tartare would be good.' They both allowed themselves a small laugh at the absurdity of this idea. It felt good to smile. The list of what he wasn't allowed to eat was so big and so endless that it eclipsed any enjoyment from food. He subsisted on the plainest food. Some boiled chicken, poached eggs, pasta, sometimes oatmeal, and always water. He couldn't drink alcohol or eat any foods with sugar or yeast unless he wanted an outbreak of fungus across his face and groin. That Frances had to cope with the daily preoccupation of what to feed him was a godsend. Sometimes they would work it out together, sharing the joke that they tried to make of it. She would sneak him forbidden foods, like bread and jam, when his mother wasn't around to enforce the Spartan regime. It helped to fill the empty hours when she read, took a drive or went for a walk. She mostly just sat, sometimes in the sun, but more often in the shade so as to be where he was, smoking, making lists, looking in cookery books, suggesting meals.

'What about salmon with new potatoes?' She offered an old favourite.

'Yeah girl, go spend those dollars, and get me some cookies.'

'Tut, tut, they're forbidden,' said Frances impersonating his mother's slight twang. 'It won't be the cookies that kill me.' His mouth twisted up, enjoying her lack of respect.

'You're not wrong there,' she said.' I don't know why you don't just say "fuck it" and have the Martinis as well.' She chatted breezily for a while and fussed around his room being charming until she was absolutely sure that he wasn't angry with her anymore. His approval was like a benediction for Frances, proving the love he had long denied he felt for her. It could still be heady when she made him laugh and some light shone in those green eyes.

By the time she had showered, dressed, walked the dog and tidied the kitchen, the non-specific malaise of the morning had not worn off, but worked itself into a tightly coiled anger that would escape in involuntary bursts. In the shower, when the water had gone all over her clean clothes for dressing she shouted 'fuck', stretching the word out until it became an unrecognizable scream. When the dog, in desperation, had crapped at the bottom of the deck stairs, not waiting until they reached the dirt track, she had shrieked meaninglessly, 'For God's sake Elmo, please don't, just stop it,' and had had to bite back irate tears. She knew she'd taken leave of her senses and wouldn't be reunited with them for at least a week; she also knew it was biology and not madness. Because her body was crying out for a baby, her mind became unhinged. Alongside the awfulness and crushing frustration of not being loved by her husband, she placed the rage of not bearing his child.

In her increasingly conservative heart, Frances saw the dangers that lay ahead for childless women, she had seen them for herself. Their brittle defiant hedonism, the transparent swipes at the importance of marriage, masking their loneliness and panic. She saw that path signposted very clearly and was anxious not to become another casualty, another woman acting like a man. Goodness knows, there was a need for a new life in this set-up. 'Fuck him, fuck him,' she muttered bitterly as she brushed her hair and applied lipstick in preparation for going to the store.

She drove the twelve miles to Meyers with the air-conditioning on max and when she opened the window to pitch out a cigarette butt an enveloping blanket of heat rushed into the car. Switching on the radio she caught the end of the weather bulletin: '. . . storm patterns moving northwards from Ohio should reach us later in the evening, but for the rest of the day, Jackson County is *hot.* Today's weather was brought to you by the John Doe Ford Dealership who have the lowest prices on all '92 models. Get down to your showroom on the Arbor Freeway today and pick up one of their great new models from only $129 a month – d'ya hear that, people, only *one-twenty-nine.*' Frances turned the dial until she picked up one of the Detroit stations. She cruised slowly in the nearside lane, enjoying the small pleasure of driving in light traffic without the need to get anywhere in a hurry. In her mind she went through the list of things she needed from the store.

Frances turned the radio off so she could pay better attention to the road signs. Last week she had been crooning along to something and missed her exit. Aretha Franklin singing 'Bitter Earth', she seemed to remember. She'd had to drive another eight miles before she could pull off the freeway and turn around. She looked up to see 'Ryder Street Exit 2 miles' as a red Chevrolet pick-up pulled alongside her. A fat blond man in a Budweiser baseball cap was sitting in the passenger seat and smiled lasciviously as he rolled down his window. Frances thought maybe he had noticed something was wrong with her car and rolled her own window down to hear what he was mouthing. The fat blond started shaking his tongue at her and screaming, 'Lick me baby!' The greasy driver joined in for a few seconds and there was much laughter before they pulled ahead and cut across her sharply, forcing her to hit the brakes. The fury that had been mounting all morning finally snapped and she could feel her blood get hot as she reached across and pulled out the plastic gun that her mother-in-law had urged her to keep in the glove box. She had said it would come in handy.

Frances increased speed and moved up close behind the truck before swerving to the left and pulling level with the red pick-up. She reached across with a perfectly straight arm, pointing the toy gun at the two hideous men and giving them a wide smile. She glanced at them just long enough to see the panic register on their faces and hear the squealing of brakes before she hit the gas hard, changed lanes and pulled ahead. She pulled off the freeway and swooped into the parking lot at Meyers where she put the gun back in the glove box, slamming it shut and complaining to nobody, 'Wankers,' before getting out of the car, smoothing down her skirt and walking across the lot to the store.

Grocery shopping had become the one sustaining activity that gave Frances a much-needed breather from 1276 Washington Drive – a grand name for a dirt road, she thought. It provided her a few hours to wallow in air-conditioned comfort, idling over the produce and making painstaking plans for meals. Before she reached the groceries, she would have to wander the clothing aisles with their plain, utilitarian workwear for men, gaudy prints for women and the universal riot of bright colours for children. From clothing, she would make her way through household appliances – cutlery, plates, irons, barbecues, vacuum cleaners and even garden furniture. But her favourite section was along the back wall of the store where they sold discount music tapes, magazines and cosmetics. There she would pick up oddments such as 'Ray Charles Sings Country', and trial-size face creams. Best of all, though, were the magazines. She would never risk the snide disapproval of her husband by actually buying a women's magazine, but she would systematically work her way along the shelf in the supermarket, reading the horoscopes in each and looking for signs of improvement in her life.

Buoyed up by celestial counsel, she would push her cart through to groceries proper. Frances always started on the liquor aisle. She had taken to buying half-gallon bottles of Blush Chablis for $8.79, which she stored in the cupboard under the kitchen sink. Ordinary bottles gave her mother-in-law a more accurate indication of how much wine Frances was getting through of an evening. And if there was one thing Meg loved to do, it was police Frances' habits and repeatedly tell her how much 'bedder' she would feel if she didn't drink. Frances thought it came from working in a doctor's surgery. 'You know honey, when Homer's father left me I used to drink every night,' Meg liked to tell Frances, 'but then I started to pray and with God's help I stopped.' It had become pointless to offer any defence or repeat again that drinking was not the cause of her unhappiness. The only way Frances could avoid Meg's concern was to lie, drink in her room, or hide her glass under her chair or behind a terracotta pot on the deck. Thinking she could store some in the laundry room, she loaded three half-gallon containers into her trolley and pushed onwards.

As she wheeled her cart round the corner into breads, she came face to face with Ginger Olson, the adulteress. Fiftyish, tall and broad across the shoulders, Ginger was a handsome, if rugged woman. She had a brave look about her that Frances assumed she must have developed as a defence against local talk. She wore thick mascara and her thin lips were a bright sugary pink. Her hair was a brittle golden colour, grey at the roots. Meg had pointed her out when they were at the hardware store in Dexter owned by Ginger's husband Al. While Frances and Meg were sorting six-inch nails for the new fence in the yard, Meg had whispered a brief outline of Ginger's affair with Father O'Connor, which she then elaborated on in the car as they drove home. Frances had noticed that for all Meg's talk of despising gossip – the justification for the keeping of confidences – she told a pretty good story.

Ginger Olson and Frances smiled tentatively at each other, joined by the invisible bond of shared experience – women who were talked about. They had never been formally introduced, but it was pointless to pretend that they didn't know each other's names.

'Good morning Frances,' Ginger said quietly, her gaze straight.

'Mrs Olson,' Frances nodded uncomfortably.

'It's a beautiful day isn't it?' said Ginger Olson shaking her long blond hair out of her eyes, the better to study the small Englishwoman.

'Bit too warm for me – at least it's cool in here,' Frances rejoined.

'I bet it doesn't get this hot in England,' said Ginger, slouching now with her hand on one hip, the other pulling her hair back over her shoulders. She liked to touch her hair.

'No, it certainly doesn't,' answered Frances, feeling awkward, wanting to talk but not knowing how, or even if, to pursue the conversation.

'So you're living in Michigan now Frances?' Ginger Olson's blue eyes were curious, friendly.

'For the time being,' Frances replied, knowing she sounded evasive.

'How's Finn?' asked the tall blonde. 'We don't see much of him, fact I haven't seen him since he came home.'

'So, so,' said Frances quietly, noting that Ginger called him Finn too. Maybe she was close to him, or used to be.

'It's a long story, huh?' Ginger raised an eyebrow conspiratorially. Frances warmed to this acknowledgement of her situation, a relief from the terse, polite exchanges with other locals, and broke into a smile.

'Stop by the store sometime and we'll have coffee,' offered Ginger.

'Yeah, that would nice. I'll see you Mrs Olson,' said Frances, meaning it. It *would* be nice to have somebody to talk to. Ginger Olson looked like she might understand. She had taken a few risks herself, or maybe just one big one. Either way, Frances could find no trace of judgement in the way she spoke.

'Call me Ginger,' she said as she glided slowly past, her hips rocking rhythmically as she walked. There was something of the burlesque about Ginger that Frances liked.

'OK Ginger, I'll call by in the week.'

'You do that honey,' called Ginger, not looking back.

Frances felt a small tingle of excitement and looked forward to seeing this stranger again, telling her their story. Maybe Ginger Olson liked a drink, or at least a laugh. In her mind, she pictured the two of them swilling wine in the room at the back of the store, swapping their stories, relieved to have found an impartial ear to bend.

She returned to Washington Drive a brighter woman than she had left it, and found her husband slouched in the shade wearing a dirty pair of jersey shorts and a tatty UCLA vest. He noticed the difference in his wife. She whistled along to the radio as she grilled the fish and boiled the potatoes for lunch, slicing up oranges and pears and melon and grapes for a fruit salad. Ostentatiously, she poured herself a glass of wine for lunch and looked defiantly into the lounge at her husband, just willing him to say something. She was ready. Emboldened by her exchange in Meyers with Ginger Olson, she lit a cigarette, not bothering to observe the rules by stepping outside. He walked slowly and carefully from the lounge into the kitchen, taking small, shuffling, painful steps. He looked at her smoking and rolled his eyes upwards in amused despair. She was easier to be around when she wasn't apologizing. He sat down and let out a great sigh of effort.

'Mom called from work, she wants to invite Cindy round for dinner on Saturday. Can you stand it?' he asked matter of factly, beginning to sort through the unopened mail on the kitchen table.

'Can *you* stand it?'

'I think it's only mom that gets anything out of that woman's company, but if it makes her feel better, I don't really care. Besides, I don't plan to be fit for the occasion.' He ripped up a letter from a collection agency requesting the repayment of a student loan taken out fifteen years ago.

'Illness has its uses,' said Frances.

'So, do you mind?' asked Finn.

'As long as she isn't going to analyse me like she did

last time. Anyway, she's full of shit, telling me I needed to "identify my blocks to growth," I mean, really.' Frances harrumphed in disgust.

'I think maybe you like it.' he said, teasing.

'Well, our discussions certainly have their entertainment value,' said Frances. 'She's a study all right, I'll give her that. Go on then, what the hell, tell your mother I'm looking forward to it.'

'Well, didn't you turn into a nice person all of a sudden. What gives?' Finn asked, studying a magazine subscription renewal before screwing it up.

'Oh, nothing, I just feel better.'

'That's good doll, that's good,' he said absent-mindedly, ripping up other bills and demands and putting them in a pile. 'What time's lunch? I'm starved.'

'Five minutes. You seem better too, I was worried about you this morning.' Frances licked the juices off the spoon she used to stir the fruit salad.

'Who the hell knows how I'm going to feel from one day to the next? It seems to change all the time. My scalp is real itchy at the moment, you know what that means, by tomorrow it'll be all over the inside of my mouth and my crotch.'

'The candida?'

'Yeah, son of a bitch.' He paused to scratch his head and screw up his face, before going on, 'And all because I ate that bread yesterday. My pee stinks like hell and my crap is almost white whenever I can force some out. It's a beautiful process,' he laughed, to reveal the generous overbite that Frances had loved so much when she first met him. The slight imperfection that had made his good looks believable.

Frances just tutted and pulled the clean plates out of the dishwasher. She'd given up making sympathetic conversation a while back. The daily litany of his complaints grew longer and there was nothing to be said, just as there was no cure for what ailed him.

'And,' he continued, lifting a finger for emphasis, 'my eyesight is getting so bad, I could only read for a few minutes this morning. My eyes get so tired, it gets all blurry.'

'I'll read to you after lunch,' she said enthusiastically, the wine starting to work.

'Hot dog!' exclaimed Finn. He liked to listen to his wife read. Despite the bad language that informed most of her speech, she had a beautiful reading voice – well-modulated, clear and just the right speed. She pushed the bills across to one corner of the table, put down the knives and forks and said,

'Come on, let's eat.'

'You're gonna have to find the divine in the ordinary, if you want to survive here,' he told her when she arrived. Mammoth cleaning jobs, she had found, could absorb her. One afternoon, she managed to while away the time it took to listen to the soundtrack of *The Last Temptation of Christ*, cleaning the bathroom. When she checked the sleeve notes on the record she saw that the running time was seventy-six minutes – a good chunk out of the slow hours that fell between clearing the lunch things and preparing for dinner. The mornings passed quick enough, but the afternoons demanded lengthy occupations. She took all the bottles of shampoo and shaving cream out of the cupboards before wiping them and putting them back. The medicine chest was given particular attention. Almost all such chores were solitary; Finn would grow impatient with her restless fidgeting and after an hour in her company he would take himself off to another room. But any loneliness she felt in Dexter at least seemed to have its purpose. 'What's good is good,' she tried to tell herself. It was a balm of sorts to have nothing better to do than go for walks, clean the house and pass what time of day she could with her husband.

On Friday afternoon, Frances was sitting in the kitchen

sewing buttons on a dress shirt Finn would never wear again. She was thinking about Ginger Olson, her resolve to go round there fading. With the distance of two days, their friendship seemed less likely. Maybe she was just being nice, Frances thought. When the phone rang, she looked up startled. The phone never rang during the day and only once or twice in the evening if Meg's sister or the doctor called. She had grown so unaccustomed to the sound of the telephone that she felt a fleeting tremor of fear. I'm going round the bloody twist, she thought as she picked it up and said hello.

'Frances?'

'Yes, speaking.' Frances tried to place the voice.

'Hi, it's Ginger, we met at Meyers the other day.' Her voice was friendly, steady and slow.

'Ginger!' cried Frances excitedly, then lowering her voice to an appropriate timbre. 'How nice to hear from you, I was just thinking about you. How are you?'

'Oh I'm just fine, thanks. Say, I won't keep you, I just wanted to tell you, I meant what I said to you in Meyers the other day. Please feel free to come round anytime. I didn't want you to think it was just blah talk,' said Ginger.

'Blah talk?' asked Frances, thinking she must have misheard.

'Yeah, you know, blah blah blah. When people say stuff that doesn't mean shit. Like, let's have lunch, I love your dress, what a cute new hairdo – you know the kind of thing.' Both women laughed. 'Al's playing pool and fishing this weekend, I wondered how you were fixed?' asked Ginger.

'Well, we've got this therapist woman Cindy Darling coming round tomorrow because Finn isn't, um, well. Maybe Sunday I could give you a call,' said Frances hopefully.

'Cindy Darling, oh I know her, she tried to counsel me and Al when we had our trouble. I'm sure you've heard all about that,' said Ginger flatly.

'You know her?' asked Frances naively. 'What a coincidence.'

'Honey, how many shrinks do you think there are in Dexter? Cindy is the head-queen of three counties. She knows every manic depressive and alcoholic from here to Kalamazoo.'

'What do you think of her?'

'Well, I guess it didn't click for me and Cindy. I find it tough to take advice from somebody who's never been married and doesn't have kids. And Al, he only wants to talk to babes – Cindy's no babe you'll have noticed.'

'She's no shrink either. I think she's bogus.'

'Oh, who knows with these people?' sighed Ginger. 'Listen hon, I gotta get ready for a doctor's appointment, but give me a call OK?'

'Maybe Sunday then?' said Frances.

'Saturday, Sunday, Monday, whenever, I'm always around.'

By the time of Cindy Darling's arrival on Saturday evening, there was no need to make an excuse. Finn had taken to his bed on the Thursday and hadn't found the energy to leave it since. His mother urged him to get up for a just an hour or so and listen to what the therapist had to say. His bad-tempered response to her plea had made her cry and come into the kitchen complaining that 'He never used to take the Lord's name in vain.' Frances had nodded sympathetically and muttered a few words of consolation. Then the dog had given his limp bark, half-hearted with age, and a shiny blue Nissan pulled up at the back door. Cindy Darling climbed awkwardly out of the car, encumbered by her girth and the stack of folders she clutched under her arm. Frances reached up and put her arm around her mother-in-law's shoulder and squeezed her gently, whispering, 'Come on, dry your eyes, she's here.'

'Hi there, you guys,' called Cindy brightly as she came

through the back door into the kitchen; she didn't feel the need to knock first.

Frances bristled at this presumption, but was momentarily disarmed by the woman's wide smile. Cindy Darling was both enormously fat and radiantly attractive. She exuded a capability and stamina that Meg had clearly found hard to resist. They had met through the medical practice where Meg worked as a billing clerk and Cindy had offered to counsel the family for free when she learned of their situation. Provided the oath of confidentiality had been kept, Frances reckoned she was the only person in town who knew what was really going on. Frances couldn't help wishing it could have been somebody else.

Meg knew the value, at least in monetary terms, of Cindy's time and was fawningly grateful. It made Frances sick to see her mother-in-law treat Cindy with such wide-eyed trust. Cindy embraced Meg warmly and then turned to Frances and gave her a sympathetic smile. 'Frances, it's good to see you, how are you feeling?' The fat lady was using her professional, compassionate voice.

'I'm fine,' Frances said, 'would you like a glass of wine Cindy?'

'Oh, no thank you. I never touch alcohol.'

'That would explain a lot,' Frances muttered under her breath. With her back to the woman, she scoured the fridge for soft drinks. 'Lemonade, orange juice, fizzy water?'

'Some diet cola would be good if you have any.'

'Sure,' said Frances, smiling to herself. It took Cindy several minutes to get her breath back; the exertion of walking from the car to the house had clearly placed a strain on her corpulent form. As Frances placed her drink before her on the table she noted how well-groomed Cindy was: the painted nails, the hair twisted up into a neat French plait, nice make-up, not too heavy, and an expensive-looking pair of pearl drop earrings. Her dress was a bright blue flowing smock and she wore matching shoes on tiny feet, above which her ankles bloomed perilously.

'Is Homer not joining us, Meg?' the professional enquired.

'He hasn't been up for two days . . . it's bad,' Meg said softly, her eyes still moist. They took seats in the lounge, a room used only for visitors. It felt weird to be there.

Frances fidgeted around in her chair, wishing she could smoke and listened while the two women exchanged information about symptoms and medications. When Cindy Darling took a deep breath and put her hands together in the praying position, Frances knew the small talk was over.

'Frances, let me ask you,' said Cindy gravely, 'would you say that Homer's physical state is affected by his emotional condition? Do you notice any correlation between his moods and his health?'

'Yes, I do, but it's the other way round. Obviously when he's ill, he feels miserable. I would have thought that wasn't too hard to work out' said Frances dismissively. Her mother-in-law shot her a look of warning.

Cindy smiled beatifically and nodded her head and said, 'uh huh', pretending to digest the words as she dismissed them with an indulgent smile. Her hands still in the devotional position she continued, 'OK, that's valid Frances, but there have been great advancements in the study of psychoneuroimmunology – '

'What's that?' interrupted Frances. She could work out what it meant for herself, but she preferred to make the woman explain.

'Well, it's the effect that the state of our psyche has on our immune systems, Frances. Patients with good self-esteem who take control of their healing often experience a significant increase in their T-cell count,' she explained.

'What does that mean?' asked Frances, understanding perfectly, but demanding that this smug woman clarify herself.

'It is my feeling that maybe Homer is blocking his progress by negative thinking. If the subconscious only receives messages of low self-esteem, then these messages will flow into every cell in the body and disease will spread. I sense that he's blaming himself and it's making him ill.'

Frances breathed in sharply. She looked at Cindy squarely, and in a patient but brittle voice said, 'Cindy, it's the virus that is making him ill, his state of mind doesn't come into it. I don't know how you can talk about self-esteem when it has absolutely bugger-all to do with it.'

'Oh, Frankie,' sniffed Meg, dismayed. Cindy nodded her head in a placatory fashion and gave Meg a moment to compose herself, before going on.

'Frances, you can make a difference to the outcome.' Frances was about to open her mouth to question the lunacy of this statement, but Cindy held up a finger and said,

'Please, let me finish.'

'Just listen Frankie,' pleaded Meg.

'What Homer is going through is quite common. Often people who face life-threatening illnesses are dogged by feelings of depression, shame and guilt. My work with these patients explores attitudinal healing, where we encourage them to choose to experience this illness as an opportunity to explore their inner natures. Also, if they are surrounded by loving, supportive, positive energy, people who have a belief in overcoming obstacles, it can really turn things around for them,' said Cindy, boring into Frances with her sincerest expression.

'Oh come on Cindy, he's dying. There is no other outcome and that is the long and the short of it,' said Frances testily. Her mother-in-law couldn't hold herself back now and began to snuffle into her handkerchief. Above her tears, Cindy tried to continue calmly. 'There are no dying people Frances, we are either dead or alive.'

'I can't listen to this! You're out of your mind, where do you get this stuff?' Frances said. 'Anyway I'm off.' She rose out of her chair. As she passed her weeping mother-in-law she experienced a flicker of remorse and made a note to apologize later. She picked her keys up and moved towards the back door, when she heard Cindy call out,

'Denial is a natural process Frances. We can help you through it.' Frances recited the Lord's Prayer under her breath, started up the engine and left Washington Drive in a cloud of flying dust that hung static in the twilight.

Ten minutes later, she stopped the car outside Olson's Hardware Store in Dexter and walked down the alley at the side of the building calling out softly, 'Hello, anybody home?'

'Back here on the porch,' called a woman's voice. Frances turned the corner and found Ginger Olson in jeans and a man's working shirt, slouched in a chair, drinking beer. Her bare feet rested on the white porch railing, the toes painted the same girlish pink she had seen on her lips in the store, several days ago.

'I'm sorry to turn up unannounced like this, I hope you don't mind, I just had to get out of the house,' said Frances.

'No problem honey, come on, sit down, can I get you a beer?' Ginger's tone was calm.

'I'm sorry to disturb you. Is your husband around?' asked Frances worried, scanning the inside of the house through the windows. Looking in, she could see jackets slung over the arms of chairs and plates and cups littering the kitchen table. A radio played in a distant room. A proper house, Frances thought.

'No, Al plays pool on Saturday, has done for seventeen years – he won't be home for hours. Come on, sit down, let me get you that beer, you look like you need it.'

'You can say that again,' moaned Frances, lowering herself into a chair next to Ginger's. The women exchanged knowing looks. Ginger walked languidly through the screen door which emitted a loud creak: from outside Frances heard the opening and shutting of the refrigerator before Ginger reappeared on the porch, pulled the ring off a can and said,

'So tell me.'

PART TWO

IT WAS DIFFICULT for Frances to recall the rhythm of her life before she met Finn, but she decided that it had definitely been without purpose. A pointless freefall through the years. His arrival eclipsed everything, pointed to a new direction and rendered her past flat and colourless. He was the big, silent surprise. There were no trumpets to herald his coming, no great fanfare proclaiming, 'Look, he's here, the one you've been waiting for.' He just crept in, noiselessly, unexpectedly, in the way the great defining changes of life often will.

She supposed she had been happy before he came, enjoying the rewards that an insignificant life yields up. She had a comfortable routine – undemanding job, familiar friends and the small surprises which made the ennui of her existence tolerable. But she wouldn't have called it living exactly. Frances always felt as if she were waiting for something to happen, not quite believing this was all there was. Sometimes she looked heavenwards and said, 'OK, get on with it. Please.' She fought impatience until finally, the shift occurred. The day she met him had begun with no signs of alchemy, but when that day was finished she knew that her whole life had been leading up to just such a moment.

It was a beautiful September day, a morning so quietly glorious that she knew as soon as she pulled back the curtains it would surely be the last of summer. She had gone back to her bed with a cup of tea and listened to the traffic reports on the radio. The Angel was completely blocked in both directions, there was little point in hurrying. She calculated that it would make no difference if she left immediately or an hour later – she would arrive at the same time. With the extra time at her disposal, she took particular care in dressing that morning; she ironed her long floral-print wrapover dress and cleaned her impractical strappy sandals. The heels made it difficult to climb the ladders in the bookshop, but she wasn't planning on doing much that day.

She had lingered over her make-up, smoking a cigarette, studying the mirror closely and plucking stray hairs while she listened to the ten o'clock news. She put her hair up, then combed it out and put it up again. She wouldn't arrive at the bookshop much before 10.45 a.m. Harry Truman, her boss, wouldn't mind – she doubted that he would be rushing either. She had often made the mistake of attempting an early start, only to find that she had to sit in Frank's Café on the corner of Charlotte and Goodge Streets till around ten for Harry to turn up and open the shop. More often than not he would be hungover and looking sheepish and dishevelled. He was hard to dislike.

Like her, he had left university with a Third in English Literature and had felt not a flicker of ambition in the intervening years. Occasionally, on those mornings when he had emptied his pockets to find that he had drunk all his wages and there was another three weeks until payday, Harry would worry that he should have taken up a career in publishing. He was forty and had a wife to prick his conscience – he was susceptible to nagging doubts. At twenty-five, Frances had few such worries. To her, the future seemed both blank and abundant – there was time to write her life's script, fill it up whichever way she chose. It wasn't too late to tell lies, tear out pages and start again. Harry felt as if he had dozed off and woken up fifteen years later to realize that his had been written by somebody else. She reminded him of the days when he was fearless and nonchalant; qualities that had left him over time, like the sheen off a fabric. She would laugh at him when he worried aloud and he was strongly attracted to her because of it.

Frances knew how Harry felt and took care to do the little things that pleased him. She would seek his estimation of books in which she had little interest, but about which he could speak authoratively. She would ask him what a certain word meant, even if she knew. She made him feel clever. By stroking his fading sense of self-worth, deferring to his opinions and teasing him just enough to demonstrate irreverence, she became a composite of all the qualities Harry admired in a woman. She cleverly exploited his weakness by allowing herself long lunches, late arrivals and early departures. She knew that he would never presume to make a move on her, it wasn't Harry's style. To be around such silent, unspoken devotion can do much for a woman's confidence. Especially one who had yet to learn of the frailties of the human heart and have her own broken.

They spent their mornings opening the mail and unpacking boxes of books, gossiping about authors, other booksellers. They would exchange aggrieved glances when a customer, or worse still, a sales representative came in and needed attention. Their preferred activity was the giving of due prominence to particular books – as if their efforts could make the difference to sales. Harry favoured historical biographies and placed them in the front of the window or in dumpbins just inside the door. When he stepped out for lunch, Frances would clear a space in his window display for the American fiction that was her fancy. On the shelves she would turn her favourite authors around so that instead of just the spine showing, the jacket would be fully displayed to maximum advantage. When he came back he would laugh and pretend to scold her, but he would never correct a display once she had changed it – he wouldn't dare.

The bookshop had become livelier that summer. Apart from the good weather which seemed to put twice as many people on the streets, the change was due mainly to the arrival of a new magazine in the neighbourhood. It had been launched from an old house on the other side of Charlotte Street in a flurry of publicity. The staff would browse at odd times during the day. Frances noted that their working lives seemed to have as much discipline and structure as her own. She took a shine to the business manager who regularly bought hardbacks and bumped up her commission. In a paperback world, she found him pleasingly old-fashioned, charming even. The editor of the magazine was admired in certain media circles. His name meant little to Frances as his heyday had coincided with her playground years. But for Harry, who had gone through university and beyond thinking the man a hero, an appearance in the shop could really stir things up. He would flap around recommending books and making bad jokes which he thought might alert the editor to the kindred spirit he had in Harry. Frances would watch amused as Harry tried to strike up conversation with the man who clearly found him a bore. Most people, even authors he admired, Harry could treat with a cool that bordered on disdain, but this one had him in bits.

The editor was a scruffy man who never bought a single book. He would come in the shop to flog his review copies. Frances had remarked that this seemed a bit mean when he could have given them to his staff. 'He's so tight,' she would complain when the editor had taken whatever amount Harry offered – always too much and always in cash – and left the shop. After he had pocketed his money, she would watch him shuffling quickly down the street towards the Venus Kebab House where he took his lunch. Often, just to irritate Harry, she would say something along the lines of 'I expect he needs the money to buy some new clothes.' Harry would stutter in his defence about the quality of the titles he brought in and how the second-hand section had really improved since his arrival. How you couldn't really expect a man of his high-mindedness to take an interest in clothing. If she really pushed it and made some flip comment about not understanding the humour in his magazine, Harry could become visibly upset and tell her dismissively that it was before her time.

After work, they spent the long summer evenings sitting on the pavement outside the pubs and restaurants of Charlotte Street enjoying a few drinks and their easy companionship. As the nights began to draw in, they anticipated the grim prospect of another long winter in London. Sometimes they would make plans to go to the cinema but these usually fell through as the drink started to work. Harry would look at his watch and talk about making a move, but rarely left a pub before closing time. Frances told him that she was becoming bored, was thinking of going somewhere. She talked of Mexico but admitted that her plans probably wouldn't amount to much. 'I suppose we've got the autumn titles to look forward to,' Harry had said. When she nodded and smiled wanly, he knew that it wouldn't be long before she left him.

That September day had been one of those triumphantly lazy days when boxes remained unopened and they spent most of their time indulging in idle chatter with their customers. Frances always volunteered to pop out and buy the coffees and cans of beer to drink in the back room. Lately, she seemed to spend more and more time looking for duties that would take her out of the shop. She was beginning to find the crowded shelves and general chaos oppressive. It was around lunchtime when the phone rang; Frances was sitting in the back room reading a newspaper. Her sandwiches rested on a pile of travel guides that had been waiting to go on the shelves for days. 'Good afternoon, Harry Truman's,' she spoke into the receiver.

'All right?' boomed her brother. 'What are you up to?'

'Not much, you?' she enquired, still reading her paper.

'About the same. Listen, we've got a drinks party here tonight for a load of Swedish architects. We're a bit short on skirt, what do you reckon?'

'Swedes?'

'That's about the size of it. Still, no worse than any other architects. Take it or leave it,' he said.

'All right then. Can I bring Harry?' she asked.

'Yeah, I thought you'd want to bring that old ligger – go on then, about seven,' he said.

'Yeah. Bye, Robert.'

She smiled as she put the phone down. She could picture her brother, probably with his feet up on his desk, making personal calls while the boss was out at lunch. Two years younger than her and subject to the same lack of enterprise, he was officially hired to sort and catalogue drawings in the Exhibitions department of the Royal Institute of British Architects on Portman Square, just behind Marble Arch. A casual figure, he applied his daytime hours to organizing his social life and scheduling in rugby practice. He was liked at the RIBA for his good nature and distinctly unacademic air. Unconcerned with either architecture or the politics on Portman Square, he was unusually easy to work with. He was fond of his sister but couldn't really work her out. Although they both worked in the West End and would meet up occasionally for drinks, they didn't have a lot to say to one another. He wished that she would hook up with a man. He thought her too fussy and his favourite description of her boyfriends was 'poncey'. They never lasted more than a few months anyway. He'd had the same girlfriend since he was sixteen and couldn't understand why his sister never met anybody she liked.

She was glad that she had put on her dress that morning. She thought it more suited to drinks with architects than her usual uniform of black or jeans. When they closed the shop at around 6.30, the sun was still shining and people were hanging about on the pavements in their shirt-sleeves drinking beer. They passed the fifteen-minute journey on foot to Portman Square trying to think of great Swedish achievements. They managed three – sex, alcoholism and Bergman. They walked into the reception hall sniggering at Harry's suggestion of staying for only one drink. She spotted her brother immediately; his big sandy head stood above the others and his obnoxious laugh boomed from the makeshift bar at the bottom of the stairs. They had arranged it so that it blocked the entrance to the offices – things had gotten out of hand once or twice before. When he spotted his sister he swung round and made his ungainly way towards the pair of them.

'All right Harry, couldn't resist the free bar then?' Robert joked through a mouthful of canapé, punching Harry playfully on the shoulder. Harry shuffled and mumbled something about not staying long while Frances poked her brother, tutted and asked him if he liked her dress.

'Not bad. Be better if you had a bit more body to put inside it and dyed your hair blond,' he suggested helpfully, 'you look like Cruella de Vill with that black hair and you know it's only queers that like skinny birds – real men like a bit more meat.' 'Real men like you, you mean?' Frances thought that her brother must have just heard that theory in conversation. It was nothing he could have come up with on his own. Robert just grinned and asked them both what they wanted to drink.

While he went to the bar, Frances studied the room whispering small asides to Harry about the crowd, which was mostly male and blond, except for the older ones who had no hair. They had the uniform look of architects, in their fashionably restrained outfits and heads bent in earnest conversation.

'Not many laughs tonight, by the looks of it,' she said to Harry.

'Does that mean we're going to have to talk to your brother?' asked Harry, appalled.

Frances looked over to see how Robert was getting on with the drinks. To the left of the bar, she noticed a supremely bored-looking man leaning on a plinth that held the marble head of Sir John Barry. His aggressively uninterested stance made her smile. He looked mid-thirties and, with his dark hair, not particularly Swedish. When Robert came back with the drinks she nodded her head in the direction of the dark man and asked him who he was.

'Get a load of the name – Homer Finney. Weird eh? Mind you, everybody here calls him Finn,' said Robert getting to work on a handful of filo parcels.

'Oh he works here with you, he's English then, not a Swede?' said Frances. She hoped she didn't seem too interested.

'American,' said her brother, pointing a finger at his head to indicate lunacy. 'He's all right really, don't know what he's doing here though. Can you imagine sorting out a load of poxy old drawings when you're a qualified architect? Must be because he wanted the opportunity to work with me.' He ignored his sister's groan and went on, 'He came over from LA to work on the new library with Slater's, but chucked it in after a couple of months. He thinks he's principled, I think he's a prat – must be earning about a quarter of what he could be.'

'So why is he working here then, why doesn't he go home?' asked Harry resentfully, sensing Frances' interest in the stranger.

'God knows what he's up to, but he wrote a brilliant letter of resignation to that wanker Michael Forbes. Sheila faxed it over for a joke, we were all killing ourselves. He said something like "You are architects, therefore you must be boring; you work for this firm, therefore you must be unprincipled; you have displayed interest in this project, clearly you are not too bright." We just cracked up.'

'He's a wit then,' said Harry, eyeing the American jealously.

'Yeah, he really fancies himself, thinks his shit's ice cream,' said Robert making a masturbatory gesture with his free hand.

'Robert!' chided Frances. 'Anyway, you have to admit he's a looker.' She appraised his tall figure, dressed in an olive green jacket over a black sweater and trousers.

'Yeah, if you like big teeth, trust you to fancy him,' Robert teased.

'No I don't, I didn't say that.' Frances coloured.

'Come on then,' said her brother, grabbing her hand and leading her across the hall.

'Let's go and say hello, he's all on his lonesome.'

'Robert, don't,' she hissed. The two figures making their way over to the bottom of the great staircase bore little resemblance to each other. He was tall, stocky and fair-haired with an open face and smile. She was tiny, dark, pretty in a pinched way. They shared a certain carefree air, but his was generous and indiscriminate, hers measured.

'Finn, this is my sister, she likes weird men. You should get on,' said Robert, before turning and walking away abruptly.

'I'm sorry, my brother's a little immature.' Frances' face burned. 'Frances Bell.' She held out her hand.

'Homer Finney,' he replied, shaking it. She noticed how soft his hand was. 'And hey,' he said, 'don't worry about your brother, it's good to have somebody to talk to. I don't really know anybody. In fact, I don't know what I'm doing here.' His voice had a slight singsong quality about it, something of a farm boy from the plains, and he smiled to reveal very white, big teeth. The top set jutted just forward of the bottom, adding interest to his otherwise blandly handsome face. He looked more approachable when he smiled.

'At this party or in this country?' asked Frances. He

laughed and shook his head. Frances felt her stomach lurch.

'It shows, huh?' he asked, fixing Frances with his green eyes and holding her gaze for a few seconds longer than was strictly appropriate. She didn't look away.

'Well, actually my brother told me that you'd come over from Los Angeles, don't you want to go back?' asked Frances.

'Not really,' he said distantly. The following silence hinted at a greater story.

'So do you think you'll stay here?' enquired Frances, caring what his answer might be.

'Who knows? I'm not looking forward to your winter though, I found the summer pretty tough.' Frances racked her brains for something to engage his interest. His eyes were scanning the crowd, she had to pull him back.

'Was that the weather or the library project?' she said knowingly.

He looked surprised and said, 'You heard about that huh?'

'Robert's indiscreet as well as childish.' Frances tried to sound disapproving.

Homer Finney made no attempt to reply, but looked at his watch and then at Frances. Her heart sank as she prepared herself for his goodbye.

'Have you ever been up on the roof of this building, Frances?' he said raising his brows in question.

'No, why?'

'I think I need to adjust my attitude.'

'I'm sorry?' She looked puzzled, some joke was passing her by.

'Wanna get high Frances?' he said. The penny dropped. Frances looked at the people in the room and listened to the murmur of their polite conversation.

'Why not.' Her voice wasn't as steady as she'd have liked, pitched a little too high. As they walked past the bar and up the stairs into prohibited territory, her brother wolf-whistled loudly and Finn turned backwards to smile at her and ask, 'So how weird do you like your men?'

That night in bed Frances went over the events of the evening in her mind, trying to pinpoint the exact moment when she felt herself transcend the ebb and flow of just living. In the few hours it had taken her to fall in love, her world had shed its imaginary constraints. The newness and unexpectedness of him filled her with hope. Anything seemed possible now. They had sat up on the roof until 11 p.m. getting stoned from a little brass pipe which impressed Frances greatly. It was certainly preferable to the mess of papers, cigarettes and ripped-up pieces of cardboard that usually accompanied the act of dulling the brain. His one-hitter as he called it was merely dipped into a wooden cartridge filled with grass, smoked briefly and put away. How glamorous, thought Frances. After three hours they finally gave way to the cold and climbed down from the roof to find a security guard who could let them out of the locked building. The party had long since broken up and the last guests had hailed taxis and boarded buses to their homes and hotels across the city. She had a slight twinge of guilt for abandoning Harry, but squashed the thought, resolving to make amends in the morning.

During that time on the roof they had sat side by side, close but not touching, just swapping stories and exchanging glances in the curious dance of courtship. Neither seemed surprised by the attraction they felt and spoke with the ease that betokens an inevitable intimacy. She had been playful, asking endless questions. Was he married? No. Did he have a girlfriend? No. Why hadn't he married? He said he guessed he'd been playing a waiting game. What was his idea of the perfect woman? When he replied that there was no such thing, she wasn't sure she had understood his answer exactly. It seemed a loaded statement. Frances chased away the doubt, telling herself she was out of it and seeing things that weren't there.

He revelled in her audacity, laughing at her questions. He couldn't recall a time in his life when he had ever been free of the worry of what others thought of him. She seemed not to care. He thought that her light touch could be exactly what was missing. She spoke carelessly, sharing her reductive philosophy of life. He played a more careful game, not so obvious, guarded even – but not unwilling. He talked about the corn belt in the Midwest where he'd grown up. He spoke of the family's modest means, but Frances noted the cut of his clothes. She could see how education had given him a veneer of sophistication, but there was a simplicity and good nature that underscored his elegance. The sadness around his eyes fascinated her, a troubled knotting of the brow that held secrets, a depth she would slowly mine.

He tried to explain his disenchantment with his life, but as he told his story it didn't seem so bad after all. She was bright, and she only worked in a bookshop – it didn't bother her – maybe sorting drawings shouldn't bother him. Maybe he just needed to get a new angle. He said he'd reached the end of the road with both architecture and Los Angeles; he was sitting tight in London waiting for an idea to hit. Waving her hands in the expansive gestures of one who has smoked herself beyond decorous behaviour, she told him bluntly and airily that he should change professions, move somewhere else, be something else. As she said it, it didn't seem impossible. Some people, no matter what the circumstances, always found life difficult and he could see that Frances was not one of these people. She gave of herself freely, did her best to enjoy life and tried not to give a shit about the rest. She was young of course and hadn't yet had time to know the suffocation of disillusionment.

She couldn't sleep, there was too much to think about, to revel in. What was it, she wondered, that made some people connect with a sense of knowing that other person well? She'd read about it, she was sure. He did not feel new and strange to her. So familiar – she could almost finish his sentences for him. He, too, seemed able to anticipate her answers, but with Frances this wasn't exactly difficult.

When she discovered that he lived just north of the West End on Rosebery Avenue and they shared a route home, they hailed a taxi, pleased at the coincidence, and climbed in, Frances feeling suddenly self-conscious. The taxi stopped outside his block of flats and when he didn't invite her inside, she experienced only a momentary flicker of disappointment. It was replaced by the greater relief of making the acquaintance of a man whose first thought wasn't to get her into bed. He kissed her, but lightly. His restraint was confusing, but she felt free of the anxiety that usually accompanied her dealings with men – of never knowing whether to believe them when they said they would call. She knew that he would call, that she would come to know him well. Luxuriating in her fascination, she finally fell into a deep and contented sleep, wrapped in visions of her future happiness.

Frances had experienced what she presumed was love several times before; in a quiet way she was almost promiscuous. But as the weeks went by and her feelings for this new and wonderful person grew, memories of old boyfriends paled into an insignificance that staggered even her. In the past she had mistaken sex for a lot of other things and was beginning to feel chastened by her new knowledge. This recognition subtly revolutionized her life, changing the inner landscape of her world. She was struck that there was about him something never quite at ease. She sensed early on that he would never give the greater part of himself to her, but for the time being, crumbs were enough.

It was as if he had silently given her the challenge to prise him open and she went out to win him with a passion. That they didn't make love in the first month of meeting only added to his allure. He would circle, come close and then pull away. These acts of confusion she mistook for charmed seduction and she became drawn further and further into him. She learned not to push and when to be quiet. She had never played the game on this level before. When finally he took her to his bed, his gentleness, respect and hesitancy made her cry afterwards. She wasn't sure why.

As the autumn rolled in, Frances passed her days in a dreamlike state, saying little. The few times she had spoken to Harry about Finn, his grim expression and exaggerated lack of interest had made her feel guilty. Poor Harry. Still, what did he expect? The only comment he made about Finn was. 'There's something weird about him Frances, watch it.' He would say that, thought Frances, and passed it off as jealousy. But Harry noticed that Finn couldn't look him in the eye and wondered why. At first she was careful not to touch or kiss Finn in front of Harry, but it was difficult.

Later, she grew defiant and would make no attempt to keep her voice down as she spoke on the shop phone, regaling her friends with the wonderfulness of her new boyfriend. Boyfriend didn't seem the right word somehow, he was too mature for that. Lover made her cringe and partner was too awful to consider. Finn. That was how she would introduce him, just Finn.

Frances tried hard to get Finn to like London, but her little escapades such as boating on the Serpentine in October or hanging out in noisy clubs were not the way to do it. The museums he liked more; especially the antiquarian eccentricity of the Sir John Soane. They went there twice. Frances would grow agitated and drift around places like the modish Whitechapel Gallery wondering where the nearest decent pub might be. She spent her wages lavishly and often took a cash advance from the till in order to buy some gift that she thought might please Finn. They trailed round cinemas and restaurants but bars entertained him little as he didn't drink. Their best times were spent in his flat, playing tapes, getting stoned and rolling around on the floor. They slept together, though he often seemed uncertain. But the one thing she could always do was make him laugh. Always. Without fail.

In early November they celebrated his birthday by driving down to Lulworth Cove on the Dorset Coast and sitting on the cliff tops watching the grey sea move around them. It seemed like a better idea than going to another restaurant. It had been raining for weeks and London was filthy – he hated it. Finn was more melancholy than ever before and Frances felt a mild panic rising. She feared he was slipping away. For the first time her lighthearted banter failed to cheer him, none of her usual tricks could crack a smile. She heard herself speak and her voice sounded nervous, her words hollow. She handed him his gift with trepidation, the realization of a great mistake beginning to dawn. He unwrapped the parcel to find a leather-bound journal, its pages blank and expectant.

'Write it down,' she said.

'Write what down?' he asked testily.

'Whatever it is that you can't tell me.' Embarrassed by her gaucherie, she studied his face, trying to gauge his reaction, but he was looking away from her, out to sea.

'Frances, I quit my job,' he said solemnly, staring at the grey waters, blue in places where the late autumn sun managed to pierce the clouds.

'Why?' She was worried.

'I'm going back to the States, I can't cut it here.'

'What about me?' she asked evenly. Something told her to shut up.

'Come with me. Please.' His tone was at odds with his words.

'To Los Angeles?' she asked, surprised.

'I was thinking maybe San Francisco, it's beautiful there and I can get work.'

'I thought you were sick of architecture, I thought you wanted to write.'

'I am and I do, but I need to earn money and I want to make a home. I'm tired of being temporary. What do you say, Frances, will you come?' She had fantasized about this moment for as long as she had known him. Now it was here a voice told her, 'Don't do it.' A clammy sweat settled around her neck. She wished he sounded like he meant it. Like he really wanted it. She hushed the voice inside her, telling it, 'It's just his way.'

'It's a big step. A long way to go,' she countered weakly, 'what if we get there and things don't work out between us, what will happen then? I'll be stranded.' Her voice urged him to ask a bit harder.

'You won't, I promise. I want to make a home with you, a life, I won't desert you.' For the first time, he looked her in the eye. In the space of a few seconds, Frances had a lucid flash – something was wrong. But having already engaged herself in the elaborate pantomime of their love affair, she knew that to withdraw now would mean admitting to an error of judgement. This she was not prepared to do. She had waited too long for someone like Finn and had already told her friends, 'this is it'. 'I won't leave you Frances, I'm too tired to move on again,' he said, looking steadily at her. 'We could get married.' He looked down at the journal and flicked its pages, afraid of her answer, maybe even regretting the question.

* * *

They stepped off a plane in January to find San Francisco sunny and unseasonably hot. The gloom of the English winter behind them, they started their new life on the West Coast with rare optimism. Frances couldn't have imagined a more beautiful city than San Francisco. Arranged on a series of steep hills surrounded by water with clapperboard houses clinging to the slopes, it looked more Mediterranean than American. She walked its streets with a guidebook, thinking that words couldn't do it justice. It was so affluent –

she wandered around the mansions of ritzy neighbourhoods such as Pacific Heights overlooking the bay, imagining the good times that lay ahead. She fantasized about furnishing a home that Finn would design for them. Yes, everything would be better now. In addition, San Francisco seemed to have an unnatural abundance of independent bookstores and beautiful people. Finn said it was a strange criterion by which to judge a city, but yes, it was a cool place.

For three weeks they stayed in a shabby motel in the industrial South of Market area on Seventh Street, peppered by flophouses and abandoned factories. It was by no means a desirable neighbourhood, but the restaurants were cheap and they could walk downtown in ten minutes. He found work in an architect's office on Montgomery nine days after they arrived. The money was good, so he felt they should free-up some of his savings. Frances spent $490 on clothes and a haircut and on February 17th she became Mrs Finney at a civil ceremony in San Francisco City Hall. That night he broke his no drinking rule and they shared three bottles of champagne. The day after, they drove up to the Russian River in a blue 1963 Thunderbird. She began to entertain ideas about destiny, wondering if serendipity had led her to where she belonged.

Finn was paid twice a month and when the first paycheck came through, they went dancing at a club on Polk Street four nights straight. They found a three-bedroomed apartment for rent in a respectable blue-collar neighbourhood on Hermann Street. There was a small park at one end of the street and a Methodist chapel at the other. There were some bars a couple of blocks away in the city's hippy enclave, The Haight, but he said he'd had it with partying for a while. He wanted to take it easy, settle in. When she draped herself across him and whined about going out, he spoke to her abruptly: 'We need some goddamned furniture Frances. Have you thought about a job?'

Frances had offered vague excuses about waiting for all her

papers to come through, but she was growing accustomed to the new and not unpleasant sensation of being supported by her husband. They hadn't really talked about it, but she assumed that once they were married she would be too busy setting up home to look for work. The second bedroom they turned into a study for Finn and though she thought the small room would make a good nursery, she kept it to herself. She sought no company other than his and spent the hours he was at work just reading and writing letters home. She told all her friends that she'd never been happier and couldn't imagine ever going back.

Finn seemed tired when he got back from work and the good mood of their early days began to wear thin. He slept a lot and started to complain about the state of the apartment. Thinking it would help, she took a job in a bookstore on 24th Street called Words Etc. The couple she worked for, Roy and Peter, were delighted to have someone with 'such a great accent' working in their store. It was just the three of them and another assistant called Susan, a bookish girl who worked weekends. Frances thought the mysticism section obscenely large, but all in all it wasn't so different from her days with Harry and she began to enjoy the old routine. Music played all day and there was a second-hand record and cassette section which became Frances' domain. Often she was allowed to take tapes home for a dollar. Business was patchy and there were great stretches of time when she could read or just stare out of the window listening to Roy and Peter talking about their patio garden: 'You buy another climbing rose and it dies, Peter, I swear to God, I'm leaving you.'

Finn was pleased about the job but grew edgy when she did her camp impersonations of Roy and Peter: 'I've got one nerve left Peter, and you're working it.' She couldn't make out why he didn't find it funny; Roy and Peter just howled when she mimicked them. She confided in Roy and told him of Finn's black moods. 'Teething problems, babe,' he would reassure her. In April, when Finn asked her what she wanted to do for her birthday, she told him that she'd like to get in the Thunderbird and drive back and forth across the Golden Gate Bridge listening to Frank Sinatra sing 'The Summer Wind'. He looked at her for several seconds and laughed so loud he spat across the room. He laughed and laughed and hugged his wife and danced around the room and told her she was 'the cutest thing, oh my God'.

That car, for Frances, came to symbolize most of the good times they shared. He became punchy when she dumped trash in the back and put her feet up on the dash, but loved the sassy way she ignored his requests to treat the car with more respect. On her birthday they drove up to Sonoma for lunch and on the way back, as the fog was rolling in, they swooped down onto the Golden Gate Bridge with her song cued up on the tape deck. She shrieked at the opening bars and leaned across and hugged his neck. As the car sped along, she looked across the Bay to the city and experienced a moment of undiluted joy. 'God Finn, it doesn't take much to make me happy,' cried Frances. 'That's good, because I haven't got much,' he shouted above the noise of the wind. Frances laughed so hard she collapsed forward in her seat and failed to see that he wasn't smiling.

As the months passed, their happy times grew fewer and they withdrew into themselves. Or rather, he withdrew into himself and she took to brooding with a bottle of wine. They spent mealtimes reading, exchanging only the most necessary elements of conversation. When she complained to Roy, he enquired, 'How's the sex?' She looked down in embarrassment and said she guessed it was a bit erratic. 'Why do you think that is?' Roy asked intently. She explained that Finn was suffering from a lot of headaches which he blamed on the fluorescent lighting in the office and was having to get up several times in the night to pee. 'Well, I think you need to talk about it, hon,' Roy said. She could tell that he thought this was not a good sign. Frances was waiting for her moment, but the atmosphere in the house was always too tense.

One day she suggested that they drive out to the cliffs at the Presidio and take a picnic; maybe there he could loosen up. He seemed to relax around water. The sun was shining brightly and the bay shone brilliant blue. A strong breeze was blowing off the water and rustled the trees behind them. The smell of pine and eucalyptus was strong – conditions augured well. Frances took his hand and said, 'Finn, what's wrong?'

'Nothing,' he replied, concentrating on his chicken leg.

'Well something's wrong.' She pursued the subject nervously, afraid of what he might say. When he did speak, all he said was,

'Oh, yeah, how so?' There was a charged silence while Frances repeated a question over and over in her mind before she got the nerve up to say it.

'Why don't you want to sleep with me?' Her voice was trembling, she sounded desperate – fuck it, she thought. He said nothing for a long time, but she didn't want to speak and let him off the hook.

'Well?' she said finally. He finished chewing his chicken and wiped his fingers on a paper napkin. Then he swallowed hard and said,

'Do you have to make an issue out of it?'

'What bloody issue? I just asked a question. It was a very hard question to ask, as a matter of fact. I thought you might take the trouble to answer it.' She was growing caustic.

'Oh shit, Frances, I don't know,' he fired back.

'Well what are we going to do about it, it's not normal is it?' Her voice was growing shrill and she was biting back angry tears. It was a scene he didn't want. Quickly, he stood up and held out his hand.

'Come on, let's go for a walk.'

* * *

Shortly after their first wedding anniversary Frances grew tired of sleeping in the spare room. She had gone there at first because she couldn't bear to lie to close to Finn and not be touched by him, but recently he had started waking up sweating in the night and she hated to feel the damp sheets against her skin. It can't go on like this, she thought, and sure enough, one day something happened. She had grown weary of watching him stare out of the kitchen window across the city as if he was waiting for somebody, and she decided it was time to reclaim the pleasure that was her due. When the loneliness of her exile had become unendurable, and her need for the touch of another could not be sublimated in another evening of television, reading, or increasingly drinking and smoking, she went to another man's bed.

He wasn't exactly a stranger, least no more so than her husband had become. His name was Luiś, he was half Mexican and a Law student at San Francisco State. He would often hang around the bookstore on 24th Street and strike up conversations with her. The only thing about him she found interesting was his interest in her. The attention was flattering. A bit older than her, maybe twenty-eight, he was handsome in that long-haired, benignly smiling and carefree way that students often are. He lived around the corner from the bookstore on Sanchez Street and would walk by most days when Frances was working and browse the second-hand section, or look at the records and tapes. He didn't have much money. Frances knew, from the way he always went away with a cassette tape that had been marked down to $2.99 or a couple of books from the 50 cent bin outside.

After he had made his purchase, he would position himself in Frances' line of vision opposite the bookstore in Spinelli's coffeeshop. He would hold up a newspaper and over it he would gaze at her. He found Frances uncommonly beautiful compared to the domestic product. Most of the girls he dated shaved and crimped and caked and polished and teased and sprayed and worked-out until they became just another fragrant facsimile of the Californian ideal. Frances wore no make-up except for red lipstick and her hair hung, glossy, clean and unfussy. She was naturally thin, but drinking had given her a small pot, the tiniest bump of a stomach which Luiś took as a sign of her naturalness and lack of vanity. And so he would sit and drink his coffee and stare at her, leaving her in no doubt of what he could do for her, if she could just find a way of ignoring the ring on the third finger of her left hand for one night.

It was a Thursday when Frances decided that she needed company. She sat by the till in the window of the store, thinking it typical, that on the very day she decided to give Luiś his chance, he wouldn't show up. The hours dragged and she began to feel tense, concerned that today of all days, he wouldn't be browsing. 'Sod's law,' she told herself flicking the pages of a magazine. Finally, in the late afternoon, around five, Luiś showed up on a gleaming motorbike, all chrome and black leather – a Vincent 69. One corner of Frances' mouth turned up in coy appreciation when he walked through the door of the shop. He sensed the change in her and smiled expectantly. He ran a hand through his hair, inhaled and stretched, puffing his chest out in the way that handsome but self-conscious young men will do when they are trying to impress a girl.

As they stood exchanging nervous anticipatory conversation, she kept wondering what she was going to say to Finn; she should call – tell him she was staying out late. No, he could damn well work it out for himself.

'Can I take you for a ride? How much time do you have?' asked Luiś politely.

'All night,' she answered, looking in his eyes to see them grow perceptibly bigger.

'You're not going home? What are you running away

from?' he asked with his affected Chicano twang. He smiled cockily.

'What have you got?' She asked flatly. Luiś put his arm around her shoulders and kissed the side of her head.

'Not here,' she said. Her heart thumped with unaccustomed desire. It had been a while.

'OK, let's go.' He walked out of the shop and jumped on the starter pedal of his Vincent several times before it spluttered into life.

'Have a nice evening,' Roy smiled and winked. He had his ideas about her husband, but kept them to himself. 'Poor kid,' Roy said to Peter as they watched her standing by the motorbike.

Above the noise of the engine, Luiś asked, 'Do you have a jacket?'

She screamed no into his ear and said that she didn't care. He protested, saying she would freeze the minute they hit the ocean highway. They would go to his house and fetch a coat. Slowly, he steered his bike the block and a half to his apartment on Sanchez while Frances followed on the sidewalk, wondering what on earth she would find to say to this man.

Luiś' house, like that of most young men Frances had known, was lacking in the comforts and order that would have made it a home. Piles of books, gym shoes, discarded clothing, ashtrays and a motorcycle helmet littered the floor of his bedroom. Frances took in the musty aroma of maleness and thought that few men were as fastidious as Finn, who groomed himself and his home with the care and attention of a neurotic woman. She missed him already, standing in this stranger's bedroom. Luiś suddenly seemed very young and unsure, his speech was clumsy and for all that college, not clever either; not like Finn. In her mind she thought, What the fuck I am doing here? It repeated itself over and over, but then he walked towards her and kissed her and she kissed him back. They abandoned the bike ride in favour of taking off their clothes, rolling around in the detritus on the floor and finally climbing into his bed. Frances closed her eyes and tried to ignore the stained linen.

Afterwards they sat in the Black Raven on 24th Street, sipping Old Fashioneds and looking into the mirror behind the bar at their reflections. Frances was aware of the space between them and the lack of anything in common beyond their desire to go back and do it all again. Luiś slipped a quarter in the jukebox and chose 'The Summer Wind'. She winced and regretted telling him it was her favourite record. She thought of Finn lying awake and looking at his watch. Frances stared at her face in the mirror and thought how her features had softened since the morning. Her cheeks were flushed and her skin and clothing were ripe with the smell of sex. She uncrossed and crossed her legs on the bar stool, feeling the wetness. Luiś talked about his family in Mexico, motorbikes and college while Frances just stared ahead, feeling quietly triumphant, and impatient to go back to the squalor on Sanchez Street and silence him.

In the morning when she woke at 6 a.m. the room was cold and she shivered under the light bedclothes. Frances opened her eyes to see swirling fog outside the windows. She rose and didn't bother to shower – she wasn't going to lie or pretend that she had stayed with a girlfriend. She didn't have any, for one thing. For another, she didn't care for concealment. She wanted Finn to know and if he was bothered he could do something about it. If not, she would no longer be in any doubt about where she stood. She slipped out of the apartment quietly, leaving Luiś lying on his back, snoring. She ran down the steps, her breath quickening. When Frances looked back at the door of Luiś' apartment she shuddered.

As she walked down the hill and turned left onto 24th Street, Frances felt a wave of homesickness, of love for London and the memory of her friends and family glowing with time and distance. She even missed her brother. The thought of them and their love for her made her feel strong and ready to face whatever was waiting for her when she walked through her door on Hermann Street. The morning sun began to tint the grey of the sky and separate the fog. On the trolley car that took her down the hill through the park, a gap in the trees opened up to reveal the cityscape of downtown. Frances had stared at this vista for many hours in Dolores Park, looking at the Bay Bridge and wondering about her future in the city. It was a seductive glimpse of the New World, all shining glass and soaring towers; promise. Although she had told herself over and over that she loved San Francisco, she began to see it as a futile attempt to cling to something that had all but died. As she put her key in the door on Hermann Street and turned the lock, it opened with its quiet swish across the wooden boards and butterflies rose in her stomach.

Frances climbed the stairs, walked the length of the hall and found him in the kitchen drinking coffee. He was wearing the thick robe she had bought for him in England to stave off the cold. He was unshaven and his face had a gaunt, ashen look. She nodded and said good morning. He just looked at her for a couple of seconds, his expression hovering somewhere between disgust and boredom. Finally, he sighed and said softly, 'Whore,' before looking back down at his newspaper. After months of walking on eggshells, trying to please him, anticipate his moods and work around him, she was ready. She raised her voice:

'Yeah, that's right, you condemn me for getting what you, for whatever reasons, refuse to give me.' Frances spoke quickly, her words spluttering out like machine-gun fire as she filled the kettle and placed it noisily on the gas ring. 'You totally ignore me and expect me not to seek comfort. You bring me over here, marry me and then just fucking leave me to get on with it. Just fuck off Finn, you make me sick.' She stomped down the hallway to run a bath. When the kettle whistled she came back into the kitchen and he grabbed her arm, pulling her roughly onto his lap.

'I can smell him on you. Who is he?' he said, breathing in the scent from her neck. Frances felt tearful just to be touched by her husband, but resisted the impulse to soften into his grip.

'Take a deep breath you asshole, he's been everywhere.' Frances got up and pushed him away roughly. The adrenalin made her feel unforeseeably strong. She banged about the kitchen making tea. Her husband stared at her, amused, pleased to see some of the bravery he thought had left her.

'Are you working today?' he asked. She nodded but said nothing. He looked out the window that faced south across the city, the giant neon sign of Safeway glowing in the foreground, the great iron girders of the Bay Bridge beyond. 'It's gonna be a beautiful day Frances, let's go sit by the ocean. Can you call in sick?' he asked, his tone soft, apologetic.

'I could, if I wanted to spend any time with you, but I don't, OK,' she answered like a piqued child.

'Please, doll.'

* * *

They drove out along Geary Boulevard, past the discount warehouses and through the residential streets of the Richmond and the Sunset districts, before taking a sharp left and meandering the car slowly through Golden Gate Park. As they drove down the speed-restricted lane, past the roller-skaters and joggers, Frances thought, 'I hate this place.' Her elbow was resting on the open window and she was staring in the opposite direction from her husband. They passed the windmill at the top of the park and turned the corner to face the expanse of the Pacific Ocean, sparkling pale blue and massive. There were still huge banks of fog which were slowly burning off, and between the clouds, the sun pierced through in great arcs. The breeze turned cool and Frances pulled her jacket closer to her. They passed the oceanfront houses, pastels of pink, powder blue, primrose yellow and lilac – Victorian wooden structures in a surreal sequence as the car gathered speed along the Great

Highway. Past the zoo, Lake Merced and the depot where the MUNI trains reached the end of the line. Above them trolley car cables and telegraph wires cast a zigzagging graph against the sky.

Finn pulled the car into the tarmacked space at Fort Funston, a craggy cliff face that jutted out above the ocean. Beneath, the wide stretch of pale sand reached hundreds of miles south into Mexico. On the cliffs, wild flowers clung leech-like in the fresh winds and the sand was blowing up off the ground. There were only a few cars parked in the lot and no-one was around save a lone hang-glider, pulling his winged frame from the roof of his Bronco. He waved and wished them a good morning. Frances raised her eyebrows in a gesture of greeting that he could not possibly see; Finn lifted his right hand weakly then pulled the rug out of the trunk and checked his pocket for her cigarettes.

He took Frances' hand and drew her towards the cliff's edge; she followed behind sullenly, her fingers resting lightly in his palm. He scanned the promontory looking for a natural dip, someplace they could shelter from the wind which was blowing the last wisps of fog from the ocean. Beneath her feet, the succulent green iceplant cracked and leaked its juices. 'Come on, let's climb down to the beach, it's too cold up here,' he said. She followed in obedient silence, not caring where she sat. He gripped her hand tightly as they took hesitant sideways steps down the steep path leading to the beach. They were careful to avoid each other's eyes. When he found a spot, they sat down to find that no wind reached them this low and for a few seconds just closed their eyes and felt the warmth of the sun above them. Finn and Frances sat in silence for several minutes, he with his knees beneath his chin, scooping up handfuls of sand and letting it fall though his fingers. Neither wanted to be the first to speak. Frances felt she ought to make some kind of apology; her fury was slipping into a vague guilt. She felt bad, but the therapeutic benefits of her night with Luiś helped to chase the gloom that had dogged her for months. At least she wasn't afraid anymore.

She looked at her husband and found him to be the same beautiful man she had first met; a little thinner and older-looking, maybe. His mouth hung slightly open and his hair fell in a thick curtain across his long lashes. If there was any hurt in his green eyes, she couldn't see it. Only the furrowed brow betrayed his anxiety. He leaned his body against her own in a conciliatory gesture and she breathed in his lemony cologne. She remembered her face pressed against Luiś' chest and the smell of his brown skin from the night before – unperfumed and sexual. She stared straight ahead at the white frothy tips on the ocean, swelling up and disappearing.

'Finn I didn't mean . . .' she started. 'I don't know what I mean . . .' The faithlessness of the previous night caught in her throat. She didn't want to feel regret, but it was there all the same. If only he wasn't so cold towards her, she wouldn't have found the need to.

Her internal argument struggled for a while then subsided into a dumb calm. She was beyond words now, it felt like the end. They both sat looking straight ahead, he still leaning against her. She could feel the warmth from his body and wanted to turn and hide in his arms. Neither of them moved. Occasionally he would crane his face upwards, just to feel the sun on his face. Along the shore a band of sandpipers chased the surf in and out before the water could catch them. Such funny little birds, thought Frances. A different day and she might have smiled.

'I get so lonely Finn,' she said.

'Yeah, so do I,' he replied.

'But I'm not the one who turns away from you, you do that.'

'Frances, I know, I'm not proud of it.'

'So why, Finn?' her words slipped out, exhausted. 'What else can I do for you? I follow you halfway across the world, just to get here and find that you've changed your mind.'

'You don't understand. It's not your fault that you don't understand.' He spoke carefully.

'So tell me for God's sake,' she shouted.

He turned and pushed her roughly down into the sand and lay on top of her, grinding himself into her belly, his throat above her face 'Is this what you want Frances? Is it? Is it?' he asked roughly between biting her neck. He pinned her arms above her head, gripping her wrists. She didn't struggle or call out, but tears fell sideways into her hair. 'Answer me goddamnit, is this what you want?' His face was red and distorted with anger, frustration, hopelessness.

'Yes!' she cried. Then she broke. Noisy sobs engulfed her body and she lay passively beneath him not moving; only her stomach rose and fell with crying. He climbed off her, shaken and surprised at his own strength. He looked at her with an expression that she couldn't read, then turned away. She rolled onto her side, curled up and lay there quietly heaving until she finally grew still.

After several minutes, he gently turned her round to face him and wiped the drying tears from around her eyes, stroking her hair, all tangled in the wind.

'I just don't understand,' she whispered.

He held her face and said quietly, 'I know doll, I know. It's not your fault.' They lay on their backs, their eyes squinting into the sun which now shone straight down on them with its noonday strength. Their breathing fell into a steady rhythm, hers falling as his rose. Their sides were touching, barely. The ocean moved in and out, washing it all away. It comforted Frances to think that as as she and Finn divided and changed, the sea would always be the same, breathing in and out. Life would go on.

A sudden noise made them open their eyes and they saw the hang-glider leaving the cliff-edge; his canvas wings flapped loudly until he was carried out over the ocean, then silence. Suspended in glorious flight he symbolized their desire to be away from where they were. The sky was spotlessly blue now and the wind had died down. The glider was lifted higher and higher on the warm currents, silently moving through the air streams, casting their hopes on the wind. Nothing more was said that day, but in their weary quiet they acknowledged it was over. Frances supposed that they would limp along until one of them found the strength to leave.

For a month after Frances' night with Luiś – who came by the shop every other day in the hope that they might repeat the experience – Finn and Frances carried on lamely, sharing half-smiles and ever greater stretches of silence. He would lie in his room reading, while she sat in the kitchen smoking and working her way through a bottle of wine. Usually she had the radio for company and would write letters home, warning friends of the split and her eventual return. She couldn't face the phone. Anyone who had kept all the letters she had written since arriving in San Francisco could have plotted a graph to show the initial high, followed by a downward progress of her spirits and the final, rude collision with reality.

Slowly, Frances tried to divorce herself from the fantasy that glues two strangers together. She wondered what had made them think they had anything to say to each other in the first place. Had she just met a man so blank and so empty of character that he could absorb the fantasies she heaped upon him? Arrogantly, she decided she had. She would listen to his movements through the walls and feel the chill of living with somebody she hardly knew. He seemed strange to her now, their familiarity was gone. In the mornings he would leave for work without saying goodbye and she would sit at the kitchen table wondering how it had all unravelled, sad that he didn't care to repair it. She still nurtured a small hope that one day he would come home from the job he had grown to hate – which would satisfactorily explain his unhappiness – tell her excitedly that he had taken leave of his senses, but could see now what she meant to him. He would apologize over and over, kiss her and take her to his bed for days.

It sort of happened. He came home from the office to find her lying on the floor of the lounge with her feet up against the wall, smoking a joint. Billie Holiday's 'You've Changed' was blaring from the radio and Frances sang along. She had lost the shy, contrite look that she used lately to earn his favour. She seemed unaware of him when he came through the lounge door and said, laughing, 'Well, looky here, we've got a party.' Frances grinned the inane grin of somebody who has been stoned for several hours and, unusually, not felt the dis-ease. It was working for a change. Smoking to dull pain of any kind just made things worse for Frances, made her look further inwards. That day she didn't care – she had reached a point beyond pain, tired of feeling tired, bored with feeling bored. He sat next to her on the floor, gently prised the squat cigarette from between her fingers and finished it, all the time stroking her hair. Looking at her lying there he felt temporarily relieved of the burden of her misery and the weight of his own responsibility. She stayed like that for another half-hour, her feet still resting on the cool, cream emulsioned walls. Through the open window a breeze blew across her face while he kissed her and slowly unfastened the buttons on her dress. Frances didn't move, afraid of spoiling the moment.

That night, they shared a bed for the first time in months, and when the phone rang at around six in the morning, Frances woke up without the usual dull weight of depression in her head. Finn answered the phone and said, 'Hold on a second will you, I'll take it in the other room.' He put the receiver back on its cradle and closed their bedroom door behind him. She strained to hear through the walls for the twenty minutes he was on the phone. Eventually she got up and tiptoed past the lounge to make coffee. She flicked on the radio – Ella was singing 'They're writing songs of love, but not for *me*'. Frances chuckled and rinsed some cups. 'Do you want some eggs?' she called through the wall.

It was a while before he came into the kitchen. His eyes were red-rimmed and glassy; his look enough for her to know not to ask questions. Frances dressed quickly and left the apartment for work. She trailed through her day at the bookstore feeling slightly sick with nerves. The hours passed slowly and she wanted to leave early, but Roy and Peter were up in Napa visiting the wineries north of the city for the day, and she had to close the store. She would go home and make a nice dinner; maybe he would tell her during dinner. After work, she went to the market, took the trolley car and trudged heavily up the hill with her groceries. She walked across the park towards their apartment, reflecting that she knew very little about her husband. Who were his friends? There were a couple of people from work, but she didn't count them. She realized that she knew nobody from his past. There had to be some, but who were they?

The few times she had raised the subject, suggesting they should get out of town and visit somebody, he brushed aside her questions, saying that all his college friends had split up and moved around the state for work. Nobody came to visit from LA, though he would get the occasional letter with that postmark. The only phonecalls he made were to his mother in the Midwest. Frances' mother-in-law had been guarded and unfriendly the few times they spoke on the phone. She told Frances of her surprise when she heard that Finn had married. Frances had joked that maybe he wasn't the marrying kind. 'I guess,' her mother-in-law replied.

'You must come and visit sometime,' Frances used to say.

'Yes, I'd like that,' his mother had said. 'But you know money's tight.' Frances had proposed that they come out and visit her in Michigan. Reluctantly his mother agreed, but Finn always had some excuse about getting time out from work.

She let herself through the door of the apartment, but even before she climbed the stairs, she knew it would be empty of his things. He was gone. Frances panicked for a few minutes and rushed around opening all the doors to see what had gone. Her alarm gave way to the relief that comes at the end of an unhappy love affair. It had never had the surety that she hoped marriage would bring. She sat down on his bed, looking at the faded patches on the wall where his pictures had hung, reflecting that he didn't waste time. On the nightstand sat a box of condoms, unopened. Frances had lain in bed many nights staring at the printed words, *electronically tested*, and crying softly into her pillow. At least he wasn't planning to use them with anybody else. On the mattress, stripped of all linen was a small cream envelope bearing his lovely script:

Frances,

I've never deliberately told you a lie, but I have withheld a crucial, and perhaps, the defining part of my life. The phonecall that came this morning made me realize that we couldn't go on. It was from a friend who told me that someone I used to love had died. That someone, Matthew, was my lover for seven years in Los Angeles. He was my first, and apart from a wild party in Westwood in '82, my only lover. During those seven years I came to hate the homosexual world and my role in it. I found it insular and self-obsessed – like nothing else mattered. I never really found the right crowd, though I believe that I did love Matthew. He wasn't surprised when I took the job in England, nor I believe, unhappy. I hadn't been fun for a long time. When I left, I had no idea that he was sick, although I think we both knew deep down that we were probably carrying the virus.

I had no plans to meet a woman, but when I met you that evening and you were wearing that dress, I was ready to live in your world. I felt that mine had been played out or had become intolerably bland next to the one I saw through your eyes. At times I felt it was only your highly romanticized vision of me which saw that which I considered most essential in myself. I'd never met a girl like you before and for those first few months, I really thought I could turn it around.

But by the time I found out that your love could sustain me no better than any man's, it was too late; we had already married. I tried to struggle on but I can never love you in the way that you want me to, the way you deserve to be loved. I think you know what I mean. I cast you as the antidote to the creeping despair of my homosexuality, tending to my half-truths and keeping my secrets. I feel now, that after almost eighteen months of trying, our ability to communicate across this inimitable distance between truth and falsehood has been taxed to its limit. I kept waiting for you to find me out, to accuse me, to leave me, but you never did, and I'm ashamed to say that I've come to dislike what I see as your ability to lie to yourself. I was thinking all along, She must know, but hell, maybe you don't. Either way, I cannot, as I thought I could, disown my homosexuality. If I had been honest with you in the beginning and asked only for your friendship, instead of indulging myself in the strange romance you provoked in me, things might have turned out differently.

When the news came this morning, I had to face up to the fact that I am becoming sick myself and can no longer ignore it. You should be OK, but take the test for peace of mind – I have tried always to be careful. It was difficult to give myself to you physically, suspecting that I was immunologically dangerous, and all the while wishing I were making love with a man. I know it will hurt you to read this, but you have to know. There's just no way I can stay here and keep up the pretence. I have put you through enough without making you sit and watch me fall apart.

I am returning to my mother's house in Michigan to consider where I go from here. There is $1700 in our checking account and the rent is paid till the end of the month – don't forget to get the deposit back when you leave. Go home Frances, there is nothing for you here. You belong in England. What you tell people is up to you. Perhaps in the end, truth is always easier. Forget me Frances, live your life. Find somebody to love you. F.

PART THREE

GINGER ROCKED HERSELF backwards on her chair with one foot pushed against the porch rail. She let out a low whistle. 'It's quite a story. And you say you had no idea? It's kinda unbelievable. I mean Frances, you're not a kid, you'd had lovers before, right?'

'More than I care to remember.' Frances winced at the memory.

'Lucky you.'

Looking back, Frances thought she had known quite a lot about sex when she met Finn. Obviously, not quite enough. The improbability of their union had yet to reveal itself then. Four years earlier she had been green enough to invest faith in an impossible situation. She knew better now. Frances had thought that if she loved him enough, eventually he had to love her back. As she explained it to Ginger, the foolishness of her notions cut deeply.

By displaying only the parts of herself she thought he would find lovable, Frances sacrificed her needs, so that she might become a perfect wife. It seemed unlikely, now, that Finn had ever fantasized about a perfect wife. Frances thought about it, taking long draughts from her can of beer. Maybe the crucial point was the stage that Finn had been at in his life. She knew that Matthew had been his only male lover; maybe after him, he really did think he could fall in love with a woman – put his queer years down to lustful adventure. Try as Frances might to see it in a light that reflected more favourably upon her, a seven-year relationship between two men seemed less like an experiment than a conviction.

'I don't know, Ginger. I don't think he was convinced he was gay when we met. It was marrying me that helped to crystallize matters.' They both laughed. 'Before that, I suppose there was always the possibility that he could be happy with a woman, or at least I think that's how he saw it. As for me, I was just so blown away by his approach. I'd never known a man who really wanted to know about me, for me. Bed always came first. But with Finn it was the last thing on his mind. It all seems so obvious now. I feel so fucking stupid.'

'He must have been scared to death. I mean he was thirty-some, right, and you were the first woman?' Ginger's eyes blazed with interest.

'The one and only.' Frances drained her can of beer, then crunched it up in her fist, like a man would.

'Well, that's something. I guess it's a compliment, but didn't you talk about the past? You know, old boyfriends, girlfriends, whatever?' Ginger fished under her chair and handed Frances another beer.

'In a way I didn't really want to know about his past. Part of the attraction for me was the intrigue, the way he was so self-contained. And surely if he was gay he'd have told me? Or at least he wouldn't have courted me. I mean, nobody keeps those things a secret anymore, there's no shame. Not to my mind anyway.' Frances looked perplexed. 'When we got to San Francisco and he cooled, I just thought it was the change and the upheaval that made him so withdrawn. New job, new city, all that stuff.' Frances looked to Ginger to see if she understood. Ginger pushed her blond hair out of her eyes and thought about it.

'Huh. Poor guy, backed himself into a corner. And so what happened afterwards, did you stay in touch after he ran off?' A long thin cigarette dangled between her lips, her pink lighter was poised.

'I stayed in touch. When I first went back to London, I kept writing to him at his mother's, but he just sent back postcards telling me that he was fine and he would write when he'd had time to work things out. He never did. That went on for another eighteen months until I got the phonecall in April from his mother saying he was near the end.'

'Weren't you scared that you had the virus?'

'No, not really. We made love, perhaps ten times in the two years we were together – almost all of it at the beginning. Then we got to San Francisco and nothing. I kept thinking that it would work itself out. For the first few months, I was just so delighted to have found a man who didn't think about sex all the time. I thought I'd found somebody different.'

'You sure did.' Ginger pursed her lips and whistled. 'I mean, did you take the test? Were you using rubbers?' She really wanted to know. Frances had found that people really wanted to know.

'Yeah, I used to say to Finn that it didn't matter and that it would be nice to have a baby. He said it was too soon. It wasn't an unreasonable argument. Anyway I'm fine. Most of the time though, he just wasn't interested. It was so awful being with this person that I loved but not able to touch him. He didn't even have to push me away, I just knew not to get too close. Do you know what I mean?' Frances asked.

'Sure I do. You don't have to be gay to not want to sleep with your wife. Why the hell do you think I went with the preacher?' Ginger's eyes focused in the middle distance, some picture in her mind. 'I mean Jesus, I must have been crazy. I thought that him being religious and Dexter being so small and all, he'd keep it quiet. I don't know what I thought would happen. I couldn't leave Al because of the kids, but he'd decided long ago that he preferred playing cards with his buddies to staying home with me. We hadn't made love for three years by the time I slept with Brendan. No wonder I was so crazy about him. I was kinda high on that for a while. You know, thinking I was the only woman. As it turned out, I most certainly was not the first woman Brendan had slept with. He confessed a lot of things in the end. At least you know you were the only woman. It counts for something.' She touched Frances' arm as she said it. 'Anyways, it all got too much for him and he started to lose his mind. Goddamnit, why is it the men who always have the breakdowns?'

'You won't say anything to anyone will you?' Frances was suddenly worried about her lack of discretion. Ginger held up her right palm and sucked on her cigarette; the end glowed in the dark and briefly illuminated her face.

'I swear to God.' She paused. 'So how has it been since you came to Dexter?'

'Well, when I first got here, I didn't think he'd last a week. Then, in the second week he had his first blood transfusion and it seemed to make a difference. He put on ten pounds and was even walking around for a while. I was feeding him up a storm the first month. Things were good, we were pleased to see each other again. But he's gone right back down again and they're talking about another blood transfusion. I can't see the point. All those drugs he takes just make him feel worse, and for what? Nothing they give him is going to change anything in the end.'

'Oh, honey, you can't take that line with the folks round here, you'd hang for saying that. They'd call you a murderer; but to hell with them – blinkered assholes. How is it between the two of you? I mean are things OK?' Ginger leaned in close.

'Mm, well I suppose so. But I feel so bloody angry with him, which is ridiculous when you consider the state he's in – I mean I should be making him feel better. I don't know what I thought would happen, but saying sorry would have been a start. But no, not Finn, not a bloody word.' Frances fussed around in her bag looking for a fresh pack of cigarettes. She must have left them in the car.

'I think the fact that he wanted to see you at this stage

means that he must love you. Don't you think?' Ginger couldn't imagine Finn not loving Frances.

Frances didn't want to think about that, and changed the subject quickly.

'What was it like?' she asked timidly. 'I mean, when it all came out about you and Father O'Connor.'

'Oh, there was talk, you can imagine. Fact is,' said Ginger smiling, 'I felt so damned good for having a man again, that I didn't give a shit what they were saying.' They nodded vigorously at one another, women in complete accord. Ginger went on, 'And these little places like Dexter are never as innocent as they seem. Seventeen hundred kinds of crap go down around here, but everybody keeps it way down. I felt bad for my kids though, it was real tough on them. They took a lot of shit at school and some of the mothers stopped their kids from hanging out with them, like *they'd* been screwing the priest or something. It was too bad. They're OK now, they're good kids. I think the fact that Al and I decided to stay together helped, though I admit, for a while I was thinking of moving to Detroit. Alone.' She lit two cigarettes from the old butt and passed one to Frances. 'I thought it might be easier for them, if I was out of the picture. I didn't think Al could live with it. But he came through, he's a strong guy. A good guy – I guess I married the right one after all.'

'And are things better now?' Frances danced around the subject.

'Do you mean do we sleep together? Oh sure, a couple of times a year, nothing special. It gets easier as I get older, I don't think about it so much. But you, you're so young, there's no way you won't meet somebody else. Why don't you go home?'

'I can't,' said Frances.

'Why the hell not, you've done enough for him? He's damn lucky to have had you here at all after everything he's done.'

'I don't know how to explain it,' Frances started, 'but it's almost as if, until he dies, I can't move on. I want to see it for myself. All the time he's alive, I feel dumped. But when he's dead I'll be a widow, and that isn't nearly so bad. Does that sound mad?'

'Well kinda, I mean you don't have nothin' to feel bad about.'

Ginger thundered on for a bit about how good Frances had been to Finn, how there weren't many women who'd come back and take care of him, and then seeing her face, softened. 'Still love him huh?'

'Yeah, in that pathetic way that people do, when they're not loved back.' Frances had become resigned to this fact of life. At least she was beginning to understand now, how it worked. But it wasn't just that – to Frances, Finn had that natural superiority and unspoken charisma that just quietly commanded respect and love. After everything that had happened, everything he had done to her and the virus had done to him, he still had it. There was no shouting, 'Look at me! See how clever I am, how gorgeous.' He had an innate nobility, which, coupled with his humility, was irresistible to Frances. He didn't have to do anything apart from be himself for her to fall in love with him. There was no point explaining to people, even Ginger – it just sounded dumb.

Frances smoked, luxuriating in some dim memory. Ginger spoke, intuiting her thoughts: 'He sure was a beautiful young man. I haven't seen him for over five years now, since he came to Dexter on his way to London, but jeez, he was really something. Just like his dad.'

'What was his dad like? They don't speak about him at all at home. Where is he?' Frances straightened up to listen. Maybe some clues here.

'Last I heard, he was living in a trailer park in Arizona with a new wife. I don't know where the hell he's at, and you'll never get Meg to speak about him. He quit the force, or got canned, I don't really know what happened. Now he works as a Park Ranger, I think. I used to date him before I married Al. He just couldn't leave the girls alone, you know the type? But he was so much fun, you know, for a cop. Typical Irish, drank like a motherfucker – Jesus we used to laugh.' Ginger chuckled at the thought. 'Then I married Al and Meg married Lou, thinking he'd change, I guess. We always think they'll change.

'Meg had such high hopes, thought Lou would wind up a Commander or something. Then he turned nasty, the way drunks always do. Mean sonofabitch to Meg and real hard on Finn when he was small. Finn was such a sensitive little guy, used to stay home a lot. Never really into sports like the jocks. I knew he wouldn't stick around here. Sure enough, first chance he had, he got on that plane and went to LA to go to college.' Ginger made a sliding gesture with the palm of her hand to show a plane taking off. 'It's a real shame.'

Eventually Frances said, 'It's getting late.'

'Jesus it's 2 a.m., where the hell is Al?' Ginger frowned at her watch then remembered her guest. 'So you think you'll stick it out hon, I mean till the end?'

'Yeah, I reckon.'

'Well, you come see me anytime, OK? And don't worry, I won't say a word.'

'Thanks Ginger.' They both rose and Ginger pulled Frances to her in a warm embrace. Frances rested her head above Ginger's bosom. She felt like she could stay there for a long time. Ginger pulled away, but with both hands still resting on Frances' arms, she commanded, 'Now you remember to take care of yourself, I'm serious.'

When Frances got home everybody was asleep and the kitchen was spotless – all traces of Cindy gone. On the table was a note: 'Frances, Finn has an appointment with Dr Craig tomorrow, bring him in around 2 p.m.' Frances fingered the note for several minutes, wondering. She tiptoed down the hall and went into her room where she put on the small bedside lamp and opened the window. All it did was let more heat in. On her bed, another note: 'Doll, mom told me what happened tonight. Don't feel bad. Your loving husband.' She traced the familiar loops of her husband's handwriting – shaky now, but still the most beautiful script she had ever seen. His little note made her feel warm. She wasn't alone, Ginger was on her side, and sometimes Finn too.

She sat on the bed, trying to work out how tired she was. Sleep would be hours away yet. She crept back out into the kitchen which was silent but for the hum of the refrigerator. Like a thief, she opened the cupboard door under the sink. It creaked horribly in the quiet of the house. Frances winced and stretched her arm all the way to the back of the cupboard until she felt the familiar glass handle on the half-gallon bottle. In order not to make a noise, she had to hoist this weighty vessel upwards – but not so far up that it cracked its head on the top of the cupboards – and then over forty-five degrees so that its bulk could be withdrawn silently without colliding with the bottles of bleach and cleaning fluids. Her wrist ached with the effort of supporting its weight noiselessly through its passage. She was almost clear. She just had to tip the bottle to an upright position as it cleared the roof of the cupboard. She had very nearly done it when her wrist faltered and the bottle banged heavily against the white wooden door of the sink unit.

She checked the time on the cooker clock: 2.30 a.m. Too late to be furtively groping around cupboards for a drink. She rested the bottle as gently as she could on the counter top and opened another cupboard to find a glass. She slowly unscrewed the lid of the bottle and with both hands supported the large container as she tilted it to pour. The pink vinegary fluid splashed heavily into the glass. Frances thought that if she were Meg, lying awake upstairs trying to figure out what the noise was, she would know that her daughter-in-law was embarking on another middle of the night binge, and turn over disdainfully in her bed. Quickly, she put the bottle to the back of the cupboard, more careless now, its glass sides clonking noisily over the tops of other bottles. By the time she closed the cupboard door, she had abandoned pretence or consideration and kicked it shut with a bang.

She walked back to her room, drinking from the glass as she moved. She felt the cheap wine sink down, not unpleasantly, onto the sloshing beer of the evening. Her belly was bloated with drink and a mild nausea rose in her throat. She sat in her room at the desk that Finn had fashioned from an old door and two filing cabinets, and stared into the mirror on the wall. She watched herself smoke two cigarettes, finished the drink and got up to go back to the kitchen for more. Finn's door was slightly ajar and forgetting her usual cautiousness and respect for his light sleeping, she opened it wide, letting in the light from the hall. She could see his skinny frame under the light covers.

'Finn,' she whispered, lowering herself onto the bed. She stretched out confidently next to him. She could feel the damp sheets next to her bare arms.

He groaned but shuffled over to give her some room. 'Where d'you go?' he said yawning.

'Ginger Olson's.' Frances grimaced a little in the dark, anticipating his reaction.

'Oh yeah, how was that? She's a cool lady.' said Finn. Frances was surprised at his reaction. Why should she be? Ginger was a real, breathing, warm woman who'd made her rightful share of mistakes. But she told the truth. He would like her for that.

'Yeah, she's nice. We chatted,' Frances said softly. She turned on her side and started pushing the wet hair back off his forehead.

'Had a few drinks too. I can smell it,' he croaked, his throat thick with mucus and broken sleep.

'Yeah, a couple.'

'Good. Can't you sleep? I thought I was the only person who liked to lay awake all night.'

'Is your mum upset?' Frances asked.

'Oh, no, she had a lovely time with Cindy after you left. They talked about your denial. They're so happy that they are in total agreement about your dysfunction.' Finn giggled quietly in the night with his wife. Stolen laughter, secret and shut away from the sleeping woman upstairs. This was when she loved him and nothing he had done to her mattered – when he defended her and made her feel good about being herself. Telling the truth was the only thing that made sense anymore.

'I thought she'd be really angry,' said Frances.

'Oh, no, she's delighted that you're as fucked-up as the rest of us.'

'Finn.'

'Uhuh?'

'Kiss me.' In the half-light, he turned his face and placed his lips over hers. She felt the dry and cracking skin for several seconds before he pulled away.

'Kiss me properly,' she insisted.

'Honey, I've got a mouth full of sores, they're bleeding. It's not safe.' He mollified Frances, but her face burned all the same.

'Sorry to wake you.' She went to get up. He grabbed her hand.

'Hey, don't apologize, I like it here with you in the dark. You know my nights are kinda long.'

'I'd better get to bed.'

He squeezed her hand and said, 'Stay for a while.' They lay easily, holding hands, and Frances could feel his body burning up. She watched the heat lightning flash in the black, new-moon sky. At the foot of the bed, the old collie snored noisily and a sudden breeze whipped through the open window.

'Think it'll rain?' she whispered.

'Oh, they've been saying it will for weeks. It's always like this in summer. It'll just get hotter and hotter.' He was wide awake now, one arm up behind his head, the other resting in her palm.

'You're seeing Dr Craig tomorrow?'

'Yeah, mom thinks I should have another transfusion.'

'What do you think?'

'Oh Frankie, I don't know. Don't get on mom's case about it though, OK? If it makes her feel better, what the hell?'

'Yeah, but Finn, it just keeps getting worse, you're beyond drugs now. The AZT makes you sick and anaemic. That toxic shit you take for the MAI gives you the trots and keeps you up all night sweating. The fluco . . .' she halted and he finished for her.

'Fluconosal.'

'Yeah, that stuff, doesn't seem to help either.'

'Got any ideas?' he said wearily.

'Finn, let go.' Her words echoed in her ears. At last she'd said it.

'Frances . . .' His voice was soft with love and exhaustion.

'Mmm?'

'Thanks.'

'What for?' She studied him.

'For not asking me to fight it,' Finn said. 'I'm so tired Fran.'

When she drove him to the doctor's the next day after lunch, they were silent in the car. The conversation on his bed the night before had had such a finality about it. Everything after could only be dressing, superfluous. 'So what are you going to say when he suggests another transfusion?' Frances asked cautiously.

'He might not.'

'Do you want me to come in with you?' Even more hesitant.

'No, it's OK.'

She knew not to push it. He was in pain, angry and afraid. She found it hard to distinguish between the two emotions with him. Anger and fear, fear and pain. It all looked the same on him. She knew what he was frightened of. And who he was angry with – everybody. Everybody that wasn't dying. He didn't want to think about it anymore. Maybe in the night, when it's dark, thought Frances, you can contemplate the end. Something in the way the sun shone and the trees moved along the highway in a warm afternoon wind forbade such thoughts. In the night there is no life, just regrets. But every morning was one day less to live.

She resisted the temptation to light a cigarette and pulled the car up close to the entrance of the single-storey white building. She had just stepped out the car and was opening the trunk when the glass entrance door opened. A middle-aged woman with hair piled on top of her head and severe eyeglasses said, 'You can't park there ma'am.' Frances just stared at her as she pulled the wheelchair from the trunk and opened it out. 'Oh, I'm sorry,' the woman said, disappearing back inside. Finn climbed uneasily into his chair and Frances manoeuvred it over to the doorway, thinking to herself how light and insubstantial this once-big man felt; how easily she raised his weight up with her foot on the back of the chair. His chair clung together in greasy strands, exposing the crude shape of his skull. Flaking lumps of scurf clung to the roots. His poor hair, thought Frances, he always had such lovely hair.

When Finn went through to the doctor's consulting rooms, Frances parked the car and came back to the reception area where she waited for the woman with the glasses to come off the phone. Classical muzak piped annoyingly, tinny in the large air-conditioned room festooned with plastic plants. The receptionist put the phone down, ignored Frances and walked into a room behind the desk area where she closed the door. Impatiently, Frances listened to muted conversation for several minutes. When she reappeared Frances noticed the garish crimson of her lipstick and how ill it suited her bottle-red hair. 'Can I help you?' the woman said perfunctorily.

'Is Mrs Finney around please?' Frances tried to keep her voice even and bright, not crabby like she felt. She was worried about the conversation going on behind Dr Craig's closed door, and resentful that she stood outside. She had no influence on the outcome of that conversation.

'Meg, in the billing department?' The woman looked surprised. Frances nodded.

'Can I say who wants to see her?' The redhead's eyes were bulging.

'Her daughter-in-law,' Frances replied.

'Surely, hold on.' The woman looked Frances up and down, before she turned to go through to the back once again. This new information surprised her.

Frances wandered round the reception area looking at the pastel prints on the walls – cheery images of dogs and tractors, children and livestock. Frances found them dispiriting. Current issues of *Time* and *Newsweek* were arranged neatly on the low, square table. She sank herself into one of the big comfortable chairs arranged around the table, and started to read about Bill Clinton's Presidential Campaign. He won't get any votes round here, thought Frances. Her mother-in-law appeared after a while, looking agitated. 'Hi,' she said.

'Meg, have you got a couple of minutes? Can we go for a coffee somewhere, I want to talk to you about last night.' Frances' words tumbled out anxiously and she scratched her head uncomfortably. Her composure was slipping. Meg eyed her coolly.

'Well I'm through in a few minutes, but then I'm going to sit with Homer in Dr Craig's office. You may as well go on back to the house and I'll drive him back later. We'll be a while yet.'

'Oh,' said Frances. That *We* did not mean we three, but we two. My son and I. Her emphasis was unmistakable. They exchanged false smiles.

'We'll talk later Frances.' Meg's eyes challenged Frances'. Her tone was unequivocal. The look on her face ended any confusion about Frances' position in the set-up. It said. 'You don't make the decisions around here, Miss, or be rude to our guests. Just who the hell do you think you are?'

Frances said goodbye and walked towards the door, her face burning up. When she got outside she hissed slowly, 'Shit,' hitting the T at the end with force. She could not abide being in the wrong and she hated these little reminders that her marriage was a sham. She was no wife who shared decisions with her husband. A child might have legitimized her position, she thought. But at best, she was a tolerated friend who could just damn well respect the wishes of the family.

Frances was sitting at the foot of the garden by the edge of the pond, her toes half in and half out of the cool, slimy water. No fish swam in the pond now. Great shiny carp used to live there, but they were bottom feeders, and made the pond look all 'messy and cloudy' Meg said, 'Much nicer now it's clear, doncha think?' she had asked Frances when she first arrived. She showed her the trees and few plants that could survive the cruel, dry summer and Frances tried not to think about England. Frances had swum in the pond and missed the fish. She'd never swum with them before they were chemically destroyed, but she missed them all the same – their silvery sides brushing past her legs.

She heard the car pull up and Meg's voice wittering

sweetly at her son, vague sounds, not words. They can just fuck right off, Frances thought. She heard the porch door slide open, but didn't turn round, just sat staring at the pond. 'Frankie,' Meg's voice called brightly, 'Frankie, we're back.' There was a hint of victory in her voice. Frances swallowed back pointless tears and turned round. She didn't bother to smile, just a wave. 'You can go to hell, the pair of you,' Frances muttered.

From the sun's low position, staring straight at her, she guessed it would soon be time for dinner. Meg could bloody well get it herself for a change, thought Frances. She usually would have had some things going on the stove, or at least cold stuff ready – some ham, salad, a jug of iced water and saltine crackers on the table. Frances had been home for hours, expecting them every time a car went past. She had no idea where they'd been all this time, and didn't want to know the intimate mother-and-son things they did together – the whispered conversations behind Frances' back. Meg's voice moved closer now. 'Frankie?' Frances turned and looked up at her mother-in-law's beaming face moving toward her.

'Hi, how did you get on?' asked Frances coldly. Meg sat down next to her.

'We're gonna try another transfusion. St Margaret's, Thursday, 10 a.m. I'll be working, so you'll have to take him. Is that OK?'

'Fine,' said Frances.

'He had some Pentamidine this afternoon, they're going to administer it once a month for the MAI.' Once a month. Frances' head spun. How long were they planning to keep this show going? When she'd arrived from London, Meg told Frances in a distraught whisper that Finn would be lucky to make it to the end of the next fortnight. Now they were planning months ahead. It was sick, absurd.

'How's he feeling?' Frances attempted normal conversation.

'Pretty weak, but hopefully after Thursday, he'll improve the way he did last time. It made such a difference – you saw for yourself.' Indeed she had seen. She had been horrified at the way he rallied.

'That's good,' said Frances weakly.

'I don't know why you're so hostile about him getting treatment Frankie, surely you want him to be well?'

'Meg, how can he be well? What's the point – nothing in the end is going to make any difference.' Frances lashed out, surprising herself.

'So what? You expect me to just let him fade away without a fight?' Meg shot back.

'Fight or no fight, the end is the same,' said Frances boldly. She was enjoying her new, harsh approach.

'Maybe so, Frances, but if it was your child, you'd damn well want to fight it. You don't have any children, there's no way you can understand.'

Meg's words struck Frances as thoughtlessly cruel, and she had to squash an urge to say, 'And whose fault is that?' Meg was right – she didn't have any children and she didn't need reminding. Slowly, Meg became aware of what she'd said and tried a different tack.

'It's all wrong Frankie, don't you see? He should be burying me. And this way there's hope.' Frances wondered if she should let it drop. No.

'But it's all false hope.'

'I don't agree Frances.' Meg hit the ground with her palm. 'Say we just take him off all his medication and let it take him – he'd be gone in a month. Then, what say they found a cure in two months' time? It would be too late. We'd be murderers, we could have saved his life, but we killed him.' The silliness of her hypothesis could not be answered – there was no arguing with a mother.

'You know best,' said Frances, patting Meg's arm.

'Goddamnit Frances, don't you patronize me. You may

be educated, but you don't know shit about watching your child die.'

'I know, I know,' said Frances in a guilty voice. Why can't I just keep my bloody mouth shut? she thought. She was stung by the truth of Meg's words, but that still didn't make a difference. Dead is dead, whether it's tomorrow, next week, next month or in six months. 'I just hate to see him like this,' said Frances, not totally disingenuous, 'I want it to be over. I can still see him like he was and that's how I want to remember him.' She knew these words would have the right effect on her mother-in-law; she was so easy to pacify.

'Oh sweetheart, I know this is tough for all of us, but when it's all over, we'll have the satisfaction of knowing we tried everything,' Meg said reasonably.

'Look Meg, I'm really sorry about last night.' Frances lowered her eyes shamefully, laying it on thick.

'Oh, that's OK. Cindy explained to me the different types of behaviour that people adopt when they can't handle their pain. Anger is your denial mechanism – it's a common dysfunction,' said Meg, confidently.

'I'm sure she's right,' said Frances, thinking, Jesus Christ, these people.

Thursday morning came up like every other morning in the wooden house on Washington Drive – bright, insistently hot and early. They got up at 6.30 a.m. in order to bathe Finn before he went to the hospital. Frances was already sweating by 8.30 a.m. She had prepared breakfast and dressed herself and was drawing a bath for her husband. He sat hunched over on the edge of his bed in the heavy candlewick dressing gown he still needed to ward off chills, even in the thick of summer. He shuffled slowly into the steam of the bathroom, his thick gown slowing his passage.

She turned off the taps and tested the temperature of the

water, swirling in some bath oil as he slipped off his robe. She cast her eyes downwards and was glad that she had not pulled her hair back as was her custom in the heat. As she lowered her head, it fell in a curtain across her face and hid the involuntary grimace she made as she caught the smell of him. Stale, sickly, milky like the old, with the sharp ammonia stench of urine that had dried on his skin and robe. She held his arm as he lowered himself gingerly into the tub, noting the shoulder blades and vertebrae protruding obscenely from beneath his papery skin.

She sat on the edge of the tub, behind him and she soaped his back. Gently at first, then with more vigour when it seemed not to hurt him. His skin felt loose, stretched and robbed of its elasticity. He lay back for her to soap his chest and arms, exposing the genitals he had been crouched over. They were grey and shrunken, mouldy-looking and almost bald, save a few long thin hairs clinging to his scrotum, which hung lost in the yawning gap between his thighs. Frances lowered her arm and washed him with what she hoped was brisk impersonality. She closed her eyes to stall the memory of the times when she had rested her head in his naked lap and taken him in her mouth; then when he failed to stir and she could sense his revulsion, she would stop. It was humiliating that he had neither cared to be sexual with her, nor offered excuses.

She shampooed the thinning hair – not balding, just falling out in big handfuls – with the strong medicated shampoo that reminded her of the lotion they used on the dog when she was a child.

When she helped to dry him, he looked like a skinny man with a big head, but dressed, he was a ghostly reminder of a much bigger person. Unaccustomed to seeing him in clothes, Frances was shocked at just how shrunken he was. But Finn's eyes had lost none of their iridescence, their greenness pronounced by the deep blue of his shirt. She remembered the shirt well, and experienced a flash of nostalgia as he rolled up the sleeves. It was one of the first courtly gifts she had bought for him in London. Had he chosen it to please her? She wondered. The hair, once thick and full, bore little of its former shine but the total look – dark hair, green eyes and long fingers – suggested enough of his faded looks to make Frances' stomach turn.

She helped him into the car, trying not to let her impatience show. Anger always followed the flickering attraction she felt for him. It reminded her of all the rejections and the nights they had spent in separate rooms. Even now, diminished, withered, needy and frail, he had no use for her body.

At the hospital she wheeled him down miles of polished corridor and shiny glass, passing nurses in rubber shoes that squeaked on the gleaming floor. The wheels of his chair glided quietly and neither spoke. They rode the elevator up to Pathology where they were told to wait. Then they were shown into a large room where men were stretched out on long brown leather chairs, all hooked up to intravenous bags on poles. Most of them were watching the Detroit news that blared from the TV. Others slept. A nurse came along and explained the day's procedure. Two units to be administered back to back, starting at 10 a.m. They should be through by three in the afternoon. Frances had watched her mother having blood taken, but never seen it given. Did the body just sort of suck it in? she wondered.

Frances sat and listened attentively as the nurse directed most of the information at her. Finn was ignored and spoken of as if he wasn't there. 'Now Mrs Finney, I want you to watch and time the inflow of blood, we may need to speed it up or slow it down. Usually it doesn't take too long unless the veins are near collapse. We'll give Mr Finney something to relax him.' Finn already had his eyes closed, with one sleeve pushed up high, exposing the map of blue veins on the inside of his arm. 'If it's taking time, we'll move you to a private room where you'll be more comfortable. Now can I get you folks anything, a soda, some coffee?'

A second nurse, a brisk woman in white trousers and tunic, wheeled the equipment over to Finn's chaise and started swabbing the inside of his arm. Finn looked at the nurse's strong hands on his arm. She prodded the veins and when she thought she had found one, inserted the needle. No blood. She tried again. He grimaced and let out a low animal groan. Frances looked at the nurse puzzled, and she responded, 'Everything hurts when they get this weak, once we're all hooked up though, it should be easier.' Long plastic tubing which hung from the bag of blood was attached to the needle in his arm. The nurse turned the valve slowly to let the blood flow. 'OK, I'll come and check on you guys in about thirty minutes. If you need anything just push the button, one of us is always around.' Frances smiled her thanks and turned to Finn.

'How does it feel?'

He kept his eyes closed. 'It hurts, but it's that goddamn TV which is driving me nuts. Can't we get a private room?'

'Do you want to read, I brought all your *New Yorkers*?'

'No, I think I'll just rest for a while.'

Frances sat and watched the TV, watched Finn. She watched the hands of the clock on the wall. A long day during which there would be little to do or say stretched ahead of her. She slumped down in her chair and started to read the magazines. One hour later, it seemed that no blood had drained into his arm, the drip from the bag into the tube that led into his arm seemed hardly to move. Frances timed the delay between each drip and reckoned that one went down every twenty seconds. Jesus, she thought.

She wandered out into the patio area behind Pathology where picnic tables were arranged and on the wall a large NO SMOKING sign hung. 'Fuck that,' she said to nobody, and lit a cigarette. The butts on the floor were evidence that other smokers ignored the sign too. How the hell can they stop you from smoking *outside*, she thought.

Dawdling, trying to kill time, she ambled back to the room where all the men were laid on their chaises. Wives, mothers, sisters and friends sat beside them, reading or watching the TV. A nurse was adjusting the little wheel that regulated the drip speed.

'Oh, hi Mrs Finney, it's kinda slow, we're going to speed this up a little, the veins are very slack. In the meantime I'm going to draw some blood for analysis. If things aren't moving any better in a half hour, we'll transfer you to a private room, so that he can be more comfortable.'

'Why can't I go now?' Finn's first words to the nurse.

'Well Mr Finney, it isn't standard procedure to put day patients into individual rooms unless they are experiencing difficulties.'

'These are not standard arms, they don't work.' He met the nurse's gaze levelly.

'I'll go and speak to administration,' the nurse said, putting on a pair of tight, white rubber gloves.

Finn's mouth puckered as the second needle went in. She drew deep, dark-red blood into the phial and looked at him. There was a shadowy hue around the eyes. The nurse stared. She hadn't seen many of these cases, but she recognized the hollow, haunted look that they all got around the eyes – the skin that turned waxy and yellow. Gross, thought the young nurse.

An hour later, having satisfied the administrators that theirs was not a regular case, they travelled up three floors and were led into a private room with separate bathroom and large single bed. A TV sat on a high bracket on a wall facing the bed. For a fee of $11 a token could be inserted in the special slot and programmes would be available. Finn was given another shot of something for the pain. After fifteen minutes his breathing had relaxed and he looked half-asleep, comfortable. 'You were right,' he said tugging her sleeve.

'Right about what?' She looked at him as if he were a madman.

'About this. It's a waste of time. I can feel it.'

'Well, we don't know that. We'll have to wait and see,' Frances said.

'Oh you know. You always know, my smartass wife.' He lay back and smiled at the ceiling. The drugs had kicked in. Thank God for morphine, thought Frances. She felt a small stab of pride that he'd called her his wife.

'Do you want to read any of these?' Frances held up the stack of magazines.

'You read to me.'

'What do you fancy then?'

'There's a good story in last week's *New Yorker* about Bobby Wayne Thomas.'

'Who?' she asked, flicking through.

'The serial killer. Haven't you read it? It's cool.'

Frances found the article and began to read slowly. There was time to kill. By 12.30 p.m., the first unit had only drained about a third of the way. At this rate they would be here until six or seven. She would read a paragraph, then look out of the window, watching the shiny cars pull in and out of the car park. She looked at the people walking towards the entrance and tried to guess what was wrong with them.

Every ten minutes or so, she got up and fetched a glass of water, or just went into the bathroom to study her face before resuming duty. Outside the tinted windows of the sixth floor of the hospital, grey clouds gathered and rain seemed to be edging closer. Inside the air-conditioned room, she read over and over the instructions on the wall for the TV service and inhaled the faint smell of antiseptic.

Frances read. Bobby Wayne Thomas left his home in Cloverdale, Barry County, Michigan at 8.30 on the morning of June 12th 1990. He drove three miles across town. There, he waited for his mother and father-in-law to come out of their house and get in the car. They always played golf on a Tuesday at 9 a.m. When they came out, he fired six shots from his rifle, gunning the old couple down. The first two shots slew them, but he wanted to be sure. When he had expelled the six cartridges he reloaded his rifle before putting it in the trunk of his car. He then drove back across town, stopping for coffee, two eggs with sausage links, pancakes and fresh juice.

He paid for his $2.99 breakfast special and drove back to his home on Pinckney Street, where his wife stood at the sink cleaning the breakfast things. She had just waved the kids off as they boarded the school bus on the corner of Pinckney and Jackson. He walked round to the back of the house and fired three shots through the window, felling the mother of his four children. He shattered the new picture window that he had fitted only two weeks previously. His wife had said she wanted to see more of the garden while she did the dishes. Just before he raised his rifle, his wife looked up surprised and said 'Bob!' before he silenced her for ever.

Frances watched the maddeningly slow drip. Finn's eyes were closed and she stopped reading, hoping he had drifted into a sleep. 'Keep going,' he whispered. Frances read again, then she slept for fifteen minutes. At 4 p.m., after snacking on an apple Danish and some coffee in the refreshment area, she came back to the room to find the first unit had drained in and a second bag being hooked up to the stand. The nurse made a few lame jokes about Finn's veins, but he wasn't laughing or even looking at her. He just lay there, sweating and pale. Frances looked at him and shivered.

At 5.30 p.m. after flicking through a Detroit paper that somebody had left in the refreshment area, Frances resumed her story. By now, Bobby Wayne Thomas had taken a picnic lunch in the park and read the *Barry County Chronicle*. From the park, he went directly to collect his children from school. The children were pleased and surprised to see their dad, and they chatted excitedly about their vacation with grandma up at her cabin in Duck Lake. They would go when school was out on Friday. He pulled the car into the drive and told them to wait there. He had a surprise for them. He walked round to the back of the car and took his rifle out of the trunk. He had stored it there, cleaned and reloaded after shooting his wife that morning. Leaving the door of the trunk up so that the children could not see him, he walked slowly round to the driver's side where he took aim and killed his children with eight shots. Not one of them called out. There wasn't time. It only took one bullet each to kill the kids. Bobby Wayne Thomas was a good shot, he often hunted up on the lakes, but he had to be sure.

Finn's breathing became laboured and every now and then he whimpered like a dreaming dog. His eyes stayed closed, but the occasional tear made its progress from the corner of his eye across his cheek and down the scrawny neck, falling into the deep hollows between his clavicle. The tissue in his hand was knotted with use. The blood bag still looked plump and full and Frances was about to look back down at the *New Yorker* to continue the saga, when out of the corner of her eye she noticed an interruption in the long red line that led from the bag down to his arm.

Not missing a beat, she kept reading, but between sentences she would look up to see if it was what she thought it was. It was. A small air bubble was moving slowly but inexorably down the line towards his arm. From there it would travel through his artery, around the heart and eventually up to his brain. She sat perfectly still and tried to work out if she was scared. It wasn't fear she felt, but a strange and calm excitement. She carried on reading, flinching nervously when he opened his eyes to scratch around the needle in his arm. 'It hurts, it itches,' he would complain. 'How long is this damned thing gonna take?' But he only looked at his arm or at her. His eyes didn't follow the tube upwards where, just above eye level, the small but deadly mass of air was making its way towards him. Not long now, she thought, and made a wish, asking that no nurses came in to fluff pillows, take temperatures or draw blood. She started to wonder if she had become evil. Could love do that?

She kept reading. Bobby Wayne Thomas' killing spree continued in its bloody fashion. Now that he had shot every member of his immediate family he walked back into the house and took himself off to his bedroom. He lay on the quilted eiderdown that had been a gift from his mother-in-law last Christmas. Then he pointed the barrel of the rifle to the roof of his mouth and pulled the trigger. Frances remembered a conversation with a District Attorney in a bar in San Francisco. She had told Frances of the importance of pointing the gun to the back of the throat. Often, attempting suicide, people made the mistake of pointing the nuzzle upwards. This did little more than leave the suicidal person very much alive but without a face. She passed this piece of information on to Finn who tried to laugh, but it had lodged somewhere in the back of his throat and never quite made it out.

The break in the thin red line descended sluggishly. It was about three inches from where it would enter his bloodstream. A nurse popped her head around the door. 'Everything OK?' Frances nodded quickly and turned back to her magazine, hoping the nurse would go away. 'Mrs Finney has called to say she'll be here around 7.30 p.m. She's working late.' Frances looked at the clock: 6.15. It was cutting it a bit fine. 'Thank you,' said Frances curtly. Another fifteen minutes passed and the bubble seemed static. Frances stared at it, but a phrase about watched kettles never boiling came to mind and she tried to hinge her attention back to the story. Bobby Wayne Thomas was dead now, the rest would be testimony from friends and neighbours. They would express their grief and surprise that such a regular guy could it. He seemed so nice, they would say.

The door opened again. A new nurse came in to explain

that the shifts were changing over; she would be keeping an eye on Mr Finney. Frances froze as she fussed around the bed, straightening blankets and checking the dressing. Then she saw it.

'Jesus Creepers!' the nurse cried, and started flicking the tubing vigorously with her fingernail; where the needle entered his arm, the dressing jerked around. Finn protested noisily, but the nurse kept flicking until the bubble started moving up the tubing and back into the bag. 'Mrs Finney, did you see this?'

'See what?' asked Frances distractedly.

'My God, if that had gone into his arm, well . . . Please, you must pay attention, Mrs Finney. Call us if you see anything irregular.'

'I'm not the nurse,' Frances accused. The young nurse stuttered.

'I'm sorry, it gets kinda hectic round here when the shifts change over. We'll be in to check more often.' She eyed Frances strangely as she left the room, and through the glass panel on their door, Frances could see her head bent in conversation with another nurse.

'What was she doing?' asked Finn, half in and half out of consciousness.

'I didn't really understand. Something about keeping an eye on the tubing.'

'Oh. How's it moving?'

'Slowly.'

Now that the moment had passed, Frances could hardly believe that she had been going to let it happen. What had she been thinking? It was too awful to contemplate. When Meg arrived, concerned and sympathetic that it was taking so long, Frances offered up a silent prayer of thanks. How would she have explained it to her? When at 10 p.m. the last of the second unit had drained into his unwilling arms, Frances was hungry and tired with the pointlessness of it all. A pathology doctor came by when Meg arrived, and explained that they would have to draw some blood in a few days. The haemoglobin count should be up, the anaemia more manageable and Finn should experience an increase in energy. 'And if he doesn't?' Frances had asked bluntly. The doctor faltered for a few seconds before saying that if this didn't work, there was nothing else that could be done. Frances thanked heaven for small mercies.

'The Sunday evening service is really great, kinda progressive for Episcopalians, I think you'll like it.' Meg chattered away in the driving seat as Frances stared out of the window. 'You know the regular communion service at Dexter on Sunday morning, well it's very traditional, but this one is much more participatory. At the end when we all join hands, individuals can offer up prayers to Jesus and share it with the rest of the congregation. I get a lot of strength from it. I think you will too.' Frances smiled and nodded encouragingly, pursing her lips to forbid the small laugh which was seeking escape.

She was amazed that she'd managed to dodge going to church with Meg as often as she had. In the twelve weeks she'd lived in Dexter, she had only been to the little wooden church twice for the Communion service on a Sunday morning. This had been mostly out of curiosity, to see Father O'Connor, the one-time lover of Ginger Olson. It was a dull, sleepy meeting that had all the comforts of the Church of England services she dimly recalled from her childhood. There were a couple of readings, a short sermon and a few old hymns. She knew most of them from school assembly. The faithful took the Eucharist, dug in their pockets for the collection plate and then everybody could get home for lunch. Brendan O'Connor could turn a service around in forty minutes – his misdemeanours notwithstanding, he was popular with his congregation. Frances had protested that she couldn't take the sacraments because she hadn't been confirmed, but her mother-in-law had guided her firmly with one hand in the small of her back. When they reached the altar, Frances kneeled down and took the wine and wafer like everybody else. Frances wasn't concerned about any religious heresy, but she was superstitious and hoped that it didn't bring her bad luck.

She didn't really know what to expect of the 'progressive' service, but from what she could bear to ask, Frances gathered it was a 'born again' affair. Indeed, when the car rolled into the lot that surrounded the ugly modern building, she saw it was distinguished only for religious purposes by the large white cross nailed to the south wall and an ugly brick spire. Frances spied fish symbols in the rear windows of the parked cars. It was a nifty old symbol to hijack, she thought. She was dying to ask Meg how long the service was going to be. She knew these evangelical types went in for endurance sessions. She still had enough residue of the manners her mother had tried to teach her not to moan before she'd even got inside the place.

The building was as nondescript within as it looked without; it could have been a school, community centre or old folks home. The only concession to worship was a modern spire, which at least kept with tradition by being octagonal, rising upwards to a small skylight, where, after tapering, the vane would normally stand. Suspended on a heavy linked chain was an iron light-fitting in the shape of a crown of thorns. It was about twenty feet in diameter with bulbs hanging down. Beneath this impressive piece of design, wooden chairs were arranged in a semi-circle around a modern pine lectern. On each chair was a photocopied sheet of hymns and a modern bound Bible. All in all, Frances found it a depressing scene, and though she craned her neck skywards towards the light, she felt that there was nowhere for her spirit to go.

A tall, slim, beaming man with red hair greeted them, and pumped Frances' hand in a welcome that lasted longer than she thought necessary. He held her gaze and his smile stayed fixed like a madman's. His eyes were predatory, sexual. Frances surmised from her knowledge of two that all American clergy must be randy. She felt nostalgic for the camp, asexual vicars back home. Meg chose the two seats right in the middle at the front, and started talking in an excited whisper to the woman on her right. She would, thought Frances. She folded her hands on her lap and hoped that nobody would sit next to her. The other chairs were occupied by middle-aged men and women who sat with their eyes closed and their hands resting, palms upwards, on their legs. They wore a look of ecstatic peace on their faces. 'Oh dear, oh dear,' Frances muttered under her breath.

She found it hard to follow the order of the service. For the first half, the lectern stood unmanned. The preacher – 'Please call me Bill' – sat among his congregation in the semi-circle, practicing a deep breathing technique, which involved a groaning Frances associated only with sexual acts. Her nose involuntarily screwed up in distaste. She found herself becoming cross at her inability to follow the service. They sang about six modern hymns back to back. It was a dirgy selection, during which they remained seated.

Bill started the reading from Romans Chapter Five: '"Therefore being justified by faith, we have peace with God through our Lord Jesus Christ: By whom also we have access by faith into this grace wherein we stand and rejoice in hope of the glory of God." Yes, we STAND and rejoice, come on, STAND UP AND REJOICE!' Frances looked at her mother-in-law uncertainly. Meg was rising to her feet, an exalted look on her face. Everybody held hands and was invited to offer up prayers to Jesus. What about God? thought Frances.

A small, frail-looking woman held her head aloft, and said, 'Oh Jesus, thank you so much for your love, for your blood which you gave so that others might live.' 'Amen!' chipped in the rest of the group. Frances' eyes widened. Through the mists of uncertain theological knowledge, something seemed wrong to her. But they were off now. A red-faced man of about sixty said: 'Thank you Jesus, for loving me, and love too all the sinners who are dying for their sins. Alcoholics, homosexuals with their diseases, drug addicts. Love them all Jesus, they need your love.' Frances stared in disbelief at the man who had said this. She squeezed Meg's hand to get her attention, but Meg just pursed her lips in a hushing fashion. 'Amen Jesus, WE ARE JUSTIFIED BY YOUR BLOOD,' cried the preacher.

Frances had now given up all pretence of joining in, and she looked unabashed at the tall, ginger man. He saw her head rise up from its position of humility and smiled. He was young, no more than thirty-five, she reckoned. When he finally put a stop to the rambling, free-association prayer, he stood at his lectern and explained, verse by verse, Chapter Five from Romans. Frances' eyes wandered across the pages of her Bible to a verse from Romans Chapter Seven which caught her eye: 'For the woman which hath an husband is bound by the law to her husband so long as he liveth; but if the husband be dead, she is loosed from the law of her husband.' She thought about it for a minute, wondering if it really worked like that.

At the preacher's side, a plump woman gazed up at him with a smile of beatific adoration. She hugged to herself the guitar that she had played passionately during the modern hymns. Spontaneously and connected to nothing else, she would offer the odd. 'Thank you Jesus' in a soft voice. His wife. Frances could tell by the ill-fitting flowery dress and white cardigan that she was married to clergy. She wore a string of pearls and wisps of grey hair escaped from the band around her head. Frances tried to imagine them in bed together; the messianic monster with the ginger hair and his plump adoring sidekick. She looked at her watch. Quarter to eight and it wasn't over yet. She shut her eyes and saw Finn's face, pale and hollow. She kept them closed to stop the tears that were gathering in the corners from escaping down her face. When it was finally over and she sat in the car crying freely, Meg reached across and squeezed her hand. 'I know honey, it's a very moving service.'

PART FOUR

FRANCES LOOKED UP at the clock on the cooker and sighed at the slowness of time. She had slept in late but yet there seemed to be too many hours in the day. The house was still; the noisy old air-conditioner had finally died the night before. The air didn't move, but she couldn't open the kitchen windows because they didn't have bug screens. The dog lay panting in the corner, his musty smell reaching her. Frances' eyes followed the progress of an exhaled plume of smoke across the kitchen and she felt faintly disgusting. Her nightdress clung damply in the folds beneath her breasts and greasy strands of hair stuck to the side of her head. She didn't want to shower just yet, as once this was accomplished there would be nothing else to look forward to.

She dragged herself up from the table and tugged her nightdress free from the sweaty creases. She studied the contents of the fridge. The top shelf was filled entirely with the pills, potions and phials that sustained his miserable life. The names on the bottles were unpronounceable and toxic-sounding. Beneath the neat rows of white plastic bottles was the remains of yesterday's black bean soup. Below that, some dried tortillas and a few limp leaves sat sadly on their shelf. Decay everywhere. She opened a large glass bottle and slugged back the remains of the prune juice, wiping her mouth with the back of her hand. From a distance she pitched the bottle noisily into the trash.

That accomplished, she slumped back into the chair and lit her umpteenth cigarette of the morning. She didn't know whether it was the nicotine or the silence beyond the bedroom door that sent anxious flutterings through her chest. Rooted by fear and expectation, she closed her eyes and prayed hard that his last breath had come in the night.

'Be sure to check on him,' Meg had called the previous afternoon as she loaded her overnight bag into the car. She was setting off to her sister's in Lansing. 'Are you sure you'll be OK? I don't have to stay at Rebecca's, I could drive back late.' Frances kissed her and told her not to worry. They would cope for a night – nothing was going to happen in twenty-four hours. 'Dr Craig gave me some more Percodan, it's on Finn's nightstand. Be sure he takes some tonight, it'll help him sleep.' Meg rapped her fingers on the roof of the car, trying to think of anything she might have forgotten. 'I'll be back tomorrow late afternoon. I've left Rebecca's number on the refrigerator, be sure to call if you need to. Oh, and Dr Craig is number seven on speed dial.'

'Go on, go,' said Frances, bossily, 'you deserve a break. Just relax and try to have some fun. Don't even think about us.' They kissed warmly. Things had been better between them recently. Since the blood transfusion had achieved little apart from yellow and purple bruising, Meg had tried to accept that there was nothing else to be done. She agreed to take Finn off all medication, going against the advice of Dr Craig. Except for painkillers and antidepressants, the drug fest was over.

It had been a substantial victory for Frances. Nonetheless, she credited Meg with the decision. She had come to understand that as a mother, Meg had to rule. She waved and watched the car disappear down the road in a cloud of dust. Frances thought she would actually miss her. She turned and went back into the house rubbing her hands. In the cupboard Frances had stashed an expensive bottle of wine that she planned to drink in peace and free from detection. She would make calls back home while she drank it.

Keeping her kitchen table vigil, she turned the scene of the previous night over in her mind. It had felt like goodbye. Maybe it was wishful thinking; she could never tell the tricks her mind was playing on her lately. No noise came from down the hallway. She looked out of the window at the length of the dirt street. The mailtruck was approaching, It can't be noon already, she thought, looking at her watch. It was. She hoped the mailman, Tim, would leave their stuff in the box. Sometimes, he came up the steps and said hello. Finn never sleeps in this late, she thought, Tim might ask questions. Her nightdress grew more sticky. When the mailtruck had passed, Frances felt relieved.

She moved uneasily, tiptoeing across the lounge to the back of the house. There were no shadows on the wooden deck and the boards burnt her feet. She dragged a lounger close to the back door, so she could hear any noise from inside. She winced at the sound of the metal across the boards. Something about waking the dead came to mind. She sat down, hitching up the damp shift to get the sun on her legs, and opened a fresh pack of cigarettes. Sunbathing like I'm on holiday, she thought. I should just go in and see. She shuddered to think of him lying there, alone. She decided she would stay where she was.

The yard looked pretty. Sunlight filtered through the cottonwoods and poplars, dancing across the bleached grass and cracked earth. It had not rained since her arrival thirteen weeks earlier. Everything except the trees looked parched. The night before, as she lay in bed, she had heard the wind whipping up and threatening a storm which never came. She'd had a strong sense of foreboding, but had awoken that morning feeling strangely calm, as though the danger had passed.

Except for the light, nothing moved in the garden and it was hard to breathe. After a quarter of an hour the sweat ran down her. She badly needed to shower. Frances pulled herself up and walked across the garden, hopping on the dry, sharp stalks with her bare feet. At the edge of the pond she peeled off her gown and slipped into the cool, slimy water. She floated, feeling the warm streams on the surface and the cooler ones that coursed beneath. Moving her limbs only enough to keep herself afloat, she gazed up at the blue sky and said softly, 'Please God.'

As she floated, she thought again about the night before. For the first time since her arrival she hadn't bothered to cook him supper. She had grown tired of preparing dishes that she knew he wouldn't touch. With Meg away, she could abandon the farce. After drinking the bottle of wine and speaking to her mother whom she had reassured, 'It won't be long now mum,' she had sauntered lazily and none too steadily into his bedroom where she fell on the bed flushed and happy. Finn had looked straight through her, staring at some point on the wall. He breathed irregularly, in shallow bursts. His breath carried the subtle odour of putrefaction.

She reached beneath the covers for his feet which were white and icy cold. Not speaking, she had sat at the end of the bed rubbing and trying to massage some life back into them. She kneaded and prodded and ground the flat of her hand into the arch of his foot. He groaned and took his attention away from the spot on the wall. For a few minutes, he had looked at her strangely, saying nothing. Finally she laughed and asked,

'What are you staring at me like that for? Are you all right?'

'It's OK, Frankie, I'm not afraid.'

'Afraid of what?' she asked.

'God has told me not to be afraid. I can leave now. Don't you see?' Embarrassed by his mortal thoughts, Frances said nothing. But she believed him. He didn't tell lies anymore.

Since he had come off medication, they hadn't talked much. There were no plans to make and he'd given up watching TV. She wondered what was going to happen to him when he died. Her only view on the afterlife was a strong desire that Finn shouldn't have one. A fear of never being quite free of him lurked in the corner of her mind. After years of diligent fence-sitting, Finn seemed finally to come down on the side of the Lord. Frances figured that it happened to everybody, sooner or later. Frances' only contribution had been, 'You're going to a better place.' She didn't really believe her words, and was appalled at their banality. She had fancied that when the time came, she and Finn would say important things to each other. It didn't happen. She was surprised to find how ordinary death could be.

'Did you hear what I said?'

'I can't remember. What did you say?' Frances realized that she didn't listen much lately.

'About not being afraid.' It was important that she believed him.

'I'm glad.' Frances patted both his feet and put the covers back over them. She sat there for a while just looking at him. For all the pain, the lies and the bullshit, he had definitely been worth it. She would love again, she was sure about that. But she would have to bury parts of herself in order to do it – the parts she had given to him that had been returned unused. Frances knew it was important to take the scene in, imprint his face on her mind – to remember. She knew in time she would forget. When he was dead, all that would be left would be his memory, and that too would fade.

She got up slowly. 'Tea in the morning then.' She kissed his forehead, tasting the salty sweat.

'Frances, listen to me. When I said I didn't love you I lied. Do you understand? It's important to me.' He grabbed her hand. She understood only too well. 'I couldn't tell you before, I had to harden you against me. I couldn't love you back. I was suffocating.'

'Stop it Finn, there's no point.'

'I need your forgiveness Frances.' It was a statement, not a plea.

She looked at him and he knew. She couldn't do it. There was everything for him in her eyes, but not that. Maybe in time, when she found happiness again, it would seem less important. But she would never forget the girl she'd had to kill in order to go on. 'Get some rest,' she said. She called the old collie to leave the room, and closing the door gently behind her, wished her last words to him had been more significant.

It seemed so petty to want to hurt him still, to use that last bit of power. She dived under the water to wash herself clean, and surfaced at the edge of the pond. She clambered up the muddy bank, her feet sliding. Not bothering to put the already damp nightdress on to her wet body, she sprinted naked across the yard and into the house, leaving a trail of muddy footmarks across the floor. Frances climbed into the shower and stood under it for an age, slowly soaping herself. She washed away the dirt and sweat, but couldn't shake the grime of her behaviour.

Frances dried herself and stood very still by the bathroom door, listening for any noise across the hall. None came. A sudden breeze blew through the house making the doors rattle lightly in their frames. She shivered. Methodically, she went about her routine, combing out the knots in her wet hair, plucking stray hairs from her brow. She massaged rich cream into her arms and legs and blotted her face carefully to remove any shine. She found the floss, pulling the waxy thread back and forth between each of her straight white teeth. Finally she sprayed herself with his lemony cologne and admired her dark countenance in the mirror. The sun suited her complexion well. She looked healthy and her mouth seemed again to have relaxed from the straight line it had been set in for months. She looked younger to herself now, as if something had lifted. As her hair dried, wisps fell across her face and she looked into the mirror for a long time, noting how the gentleness seemed to be returning to her features.

As she put on her make-up, she started to think about the future. It stretched blank and empty ahead of her. It had seemed pointless before, to look ahead, when he was still around. For the first time she imagined herself safe from him. She tried to shake off the the stigma of his betrayal and stand up straight again. She wondered if she would be able to cry at his funeral or whether relief would overshadow her grief. Frances wrapped herself in her lilac print dress, the one she had worn the day they met, its silky fabric falling coolly around her. Its crossover style exposed her legs as she walked and she became aware of her attractiveness as it might appear in the eyes of other men. She had long since given up trying to be attractive for him.

Frances wondered if, in the space created by unrequited love, a badness had rushed in to fill up the void. She knew there was a particular type of evil that inhabited certain women. The ones who gave their love only to have it given back to them. She wondered if she was now one of those women. She felt unclean and knew that her chances of finding simple, uncomplicated happiness again were slim. She couldn't pinpoint the exact moment when her need for revenge had supplanted her love for him. In colluding with his deceit, she had created so many layers that she couldn't find her way out. What had actually happened between them was lost even to memory. She looked at her watch – 1.30 p.m. Walking out of the house she looked back only to call for the dog, 'Come on Elmo.'

She walked the half mile to the end of Washington, where the dirt road trailed into a path that bisected the cornfields. She enjoyed the picture she had in her mind: of herself striding away from the house, and her past. On one side the corn had been cut, leaving brittle stalks. But on the other it remained high, as tall as she was, and the dog ran and disappeared. Where the path widened and brought her onto the two-lane Huron Highway, she waited for a truck to pass and the dog to catch up before crossing over and continuing along the unpaved dirt road on the other side. She stopped to take off the flimsy sandals she thought suited her dress, and continued in bare feet. Her dress trailed behind her slightly in a breeze which was picking up. The clouds seemed to move together and join up, creating a carpet of grey above her. The sun, for several minutes, struggled like a searchlight through the clouds, filtering light randomly, until there were no gaps left and it disappeared completely.

She walked for a couple of miles, thinking she should turn back but finding the prospect of yet more distance between herself and Finn irresistible. She passed fields with horses and modest ranch-style homes with their rusting bicycles and peeling-paint barns. A line of high trees parted to reveal a smarter house with a large white fence surrounding it. In the driveway sat an old powder-blue Chevrolet. The hood was up and two large dogs lay asleep beside it. The old collie bounded up the drive to make friends. Frances called to the dog but he ignored her. The sound of her voice caused a man to lift his head up from under the hood of the truck where he was working. He was tall and rangy with light brown hair that covered his eyes. He wasn't wearing a shirt. 'Come on Elmo!' she called. She raised her hand to the man and shouted, 'Sorry.' He waved back and said it was no problem, laughing at the three dogs.

She walked on, but slowed a little way ahead to turn and appreciate the back view of the strong, tall man. For a moment Frances imagined what it would be like to lie beneath him, her legs curled around his back, his full weight on her. Something stirred and she recognized it as desire. Her body began to tingle with the exertion of the walk and her stride lengthened, parting her legs further with each step. In her mind, she saw faceless bodies and herself between them, sliding, pulled this way and that. Hands everywhere and stomachs slick with sweat. She felt bigger and found herself taking deep gulps of air, her breath quickening.

A flash of lightning lit up the grey and Frances stopped to wait for the thunder. When it came it boomed across the plains and she looked upwards, expecting to see Finn ascending. She stayed like that for a while and enjoyed the first, warm, heavy drops of rain on her face. Frances felt a tight hand at the back of her neck release its grip. She rolled her head from side to side, not believing the new freedom. She shivered in the wet and knew she had to head for home. She called the dog and they sat beneath a tree while she refastened her shoes. The old dog nuzzled into her flank, trembling slightly at the thunder. She cupped the dog's grey muzzle in her hand and said, 'It's OK, he's gone now. Come on, let's make a run for it.'

Frances' shoes pinched, the heels beginning to sink into the softening ground. The rain was still fairly light, but as she closed in on it, she could see the blackest clouds gathered over the house. The rain grew thicker as she moved and a wind started to whistle down the cornfields. Frances ran the final half a mile with increasing speed, feeling a terrible anxiety. She was soaked through and her dress stuck to her legs, restricting her. She shouldn't have gone so far. This was weather on a scale Frances had never encountered before, and she suddenly woke up to the fear. The dog stopped and whined piteously, shaking. Frances dragged him to the corner of Washington. 'Come on, Elmo, it's not far.'

When she reached the house, Frances ran up the steps and closed the door behind her. She leaned against it, dripping on the floor. The dog was panting hard and shook himself, casting muddy drops of water and pawprints across the gleaming tile of the floor. She went to get a towel to wipe the dog, but suddenly stopped. As her breathing slowed she noticed an odour and, inhaling deeply, recognized the smell as brewing coffee. Nervous bile rose up in her throat. In the few seconds it took her to cross the hallway and enter the kitchen, her mind conjured an image of her mother-in-law sitting at the table. Back early from Lansing. She had sensed what was happening and was waiting for Frances. Waiting for an explanation. In her panic, Frances' mind went blank.

He was drinking a cup of coffee. In a slow-motion moment and with shaking hands, he pulled a cup to his lips. She watched as he carefully set the cup back on the saucer with both hands before looking up at her. Their eyes met expressionlessly, then he spoke. In the perfect silence, his words, uttered so slowly, seemed to go on and on: 'I'm sorry, . . . I'm sorry, . . . I'm so sorry . . .'

Frances thought how beautiful he looked and noticed, as if for the first time, how green his eyes were. 'Yeah, me too.'